HADLEY

The First Mrs. Hemingway

Also by Alice Hunt Sokoloff

COSIMA WAGNER: EXTRAORDINARY DAUGHTER
OF FRANZ LISZT

KATE CHASE FOR THE DEFENSE

HADLEY
The First Mrs. Hemingway

ALICE HUNT SOKOLOFF

ILLUSTRATED WITH PHOTOGRAPHS

DODD, MEAD & COMPANY

NEW YORK

ACKNOWLEDGMENTS

This book is based on the recollections of Hadley Hemingway Mowrer given to the author in many dozen personal interviews over a period of nearly two years, and also on the more than one hundred of her letters to Ernest Hemingway which she made available. Unfortunately, his letters to her of the same period have been lost. She has been most kind in granting permission to use her invaluable collection of family photographs. It is with deep affection and esteem that I should like to express my gratitude to her for her time and effort and always willing cooperation.

I should like to add my grateful thanks to Dr. Carlos Baker, not only for the interest of his remarkable biography of Ernest Hemingway, but for his generous help in making material available to me. I am most grateful also to Mrs. Ernest J. Miller for making available letters from Hadley to Mrs. C. E. Hemingway, and to Lillian T. Mowrer, Mrs. Archibald MacLeish, and Lewis Galantière for their kind response to my inquiries.

—Alice Hunt Sokoloff

ILLUSTRATIONS

HADLEY

The First Mrs. Hemingway

CHAPTER

I

Nothing in Elizabeth Hadley Richardson's early background
had prepared her for the originality, the excitement, the rawness,
vigor, and novelty of the man world she entered with Ernest
Hemingway. Coming from a quiet, conservative St. Louis family
she had never dreamed of such a life, but she threw herself into
it with not a backward glance. As she wrote Ernest once while
they were engaged: "The world's a jail and we're going to break
it together." [1]

Hadley, born in St. Louis, November 9, 1891, was the youngest of six children of James and Florence Richardson. Two of
these children died in infancy before Hadley and her sister Florence, always known as Fonnie, were born. Fonnie was only
twenty-two months older than Hadley but there was a big gap
in age between the two little girls and their older brother, Jamie,
and sister, Dorothea. Jamie was twelve years older and already
too much a young man to pay very much attention to his little
sisters, but Hadley and Dorothea, in spite of nearly eleven years
difference in age, were very close.

In many ways, Hadley's upbringing was thoroughly conventional. She attended an exclusive school, went to the best dancing
class, and had all the right friends. Everything was most correct.

But although Mrs. Richardson saw to it that her children had the proper bringing up, as she herself had had, she was far from being merely a conventional society woman. Her overriding interest, which consumed her attention and energy all her life, was in the exploration of all kinds of religious beliefs. She studied theosophy and mental science and was intensely interested in psychic phenomena. She had a strong and searching mind which was not satisfied with easy answers or accepted dogmas. A free and independent thinker, a woman of strong personality and convictions, she was the dominant influence in the Richardson family.

James Richardson was a far more gentle spirit. He had great charm and humor but lacked the drive and stamina to make a success in the business world. He had, perhaps, felt overshadowed by his father, James Richardson, Sr., who had moved to St. Louis from Hopkinton, New Hampshire. Mr. Richardson, Sr. had been active in the cultural and intellectual life of St. Louis and was one of the founders of the symphony orchestra there. A successful banker, he later established the Richardson Drug Company. A man of force and ability, he quickly achieved a position of considerable prominence. His son, Hadley's father, dutifully entered the family pharmaceutical house but hardly found it congenial.

The family home in St. Louis was a roomy, comfortable old house surrounded by oak trees and fine lawn. It was in the West End, on Cabanné Place which was nearly out in the country in those days. Hadley still dreams occasionally of that house with its wide porch where she used to swing, the paneled staircase with the secret panel, and the red glass, gleaming with the afternoon sun, in the window over the window seat. In addition to her interest in religion, Mrs. Richardson was an accomplished pianist. There were two Steinway grand pianos in the yellow music room where she and a group of friends would play regularly symphonies, concertos, and two-piano literature. In the evening she would often accompany while her husband sang, and Hadley remembers lying in bed in the nursery and being lulled to sleep by the sound of her father's fine baritone voice.

Hadley was an impulsive, affectionate girl who loved people and was completely at ease with them. She had red hair and vivid blue eyes and was extremely talkative. One day her impulsiveness resulted in an accident that could well have crippled her for life. She was in the second floor nursery, talking out of the window with Mike, the handyman, of whom she was very fond. Forgetting in her enthusiasm where she was, she leaned too far out, lost her balance and fell onto the brick walk along the side of the house. Almost miraculously she was not critically injured, although she did suffer a back injury which was to give her trouble on and off for the rest of her life. It was a long time before she could walk again and for months she had to be wheeled about in a little carriage.

Each summer Mrs. Richardson would take her family East to escape the heat of St. Louis summers. Her father, Edward Wyman, who had founded a boys' school in St. Louis, had been born in Medford, Massachusetts, so it is not surprising that the family retained a close connection with New England. Hadley's first memory is of a hotel in Maine, Green Acres, run by a religious group in which Mrs. Richardson was interested at that time. Later summers they went to Rye Beach in New Hampshire. There were always plenty of children to play with but Mrs. Richardson was extremely strict about not letting Hadley and Fonnie swim unless the temperature of the water was at least seventy-two degrees. Perhaps it was due to Hadley's back injury that Mrs. Richardson was especially cautious about her going into the water; the result was that it was years before Hadley learned to swim at all, and she never really conquered her fear of the water.

In late summer Mr. Richardson would join the family and then they would go to the White Mountains to an old hotel that is still there, Pendexter Mansion. Mr. Richardson would take his two daughters on long hikes, and although Hadley was a little in awe of him, she enjoyed his company, especially on vacations. He had a great sense of humor and so did Hadley, who has always thought life would be rather pointless if you could not laugh.

In St. Louis the girls attended the Mary Institute, a private school for girls where their mother had also been a pupil. Hadley liked everything about the school except mathematics. She made friends easily and enjoyed the companionship of her schoolmates. She had been very disappointed earlier when her mother took her out of Sunday school because she thought the child was being taught all wrong. But Mrs. Richardson was inflexible. Although she herself had been brought up as a Presbyterian, she was dead set against formal church-going.

With Mrs. Richardson's interest in music she saw to it that the girls started piano lessons at an early age. Hadley was especially responsive and soon showed a considerable talent. She preferred playing the piano to practicing but her teachers were strict and managed to give her a sound technical foundation. They were two young women, Miss Miller and Miss Schaefer, who had studied music in Germany and had come home and set up a music school. It was Miss Schaefer who later suggested that Hadley ought to go to Germany and study piano seriously. Hadley was excited at the idea of such a possibility, and the prospect stayed in her mind for years.

Her older brother and sister, Jamie and Dorothea, had a great many friends who came often to the house. There were dances, with a small dance band playing on the landing of the staircase. There were evenings of singing with Mrs. Richardson accompanying at the piano. There were quiet family sessions of reading aloud, and Hadley especially enjoyed Dickens. It all seemed agreeable and secure, but it was not to last long. Financial reverses made it necessary to move to a smaller house, also on Cabanné Place, and it was there, when Hadley was twelve years old, that her father took his life.

Jamie was already married by that time and living in Omaha, as the family pharmaceutical house had been moved there. Dorothea too was married but living just outside St. Louis in the country, and as always she was a great comfort to Hadley, though Hadley was a little too young to feel the full impact of the tragedy of her father's death.

Hadley has only dim memories of her father. Had he lived longer she would undoubtedly have developed a close and understanding relationship with him which might have spared her some of the difficulties that were to come in her adolescent years. And he might have found in his youngest daughter a release for some of the dark forces which led to his ultimate tragedy. He was a sensitive man who was not able to withstand the pressures of business and of life. A few years before his death he had started drinking heavily, something of which Mrs. Richardson thoroughly disapproved and this undoubtedly was a source of friction between them. It was from her father that Hadley inherited her wry sense of humor, a kind of humor not shared by her mother or her sister Fonnie. Fonnie and her mother were to develop an ever increasing closeness as the years went by. Mrs. Richardson seemed to understand this brunette daughter far better than she did her red-haired youngest child, and none of the conflicts developed with Fonnie that later came between Hadley and her mother.

After her husband's death, Mrs. Richardson decided to move once again, this time to a small frame house on Cates Avenue to which she added a comfortable brick wing. This house was to remain the family home from then on. In summers Mrs. Richardson continued to take her two young daughters East to a house she had built at Annisquam, not far from Gloucester, on Ipswich Bay. It was on a lovely point of land near the lighthouse, surrounded by sand dunes and looking out over the bay.

But there were none of the dancing or singing parties for Hadley and Fonnie that there had been for the older children. Mrs. Richardson's interest in theosophy and mental science began to absorb more and more of her time. She had a circle of friends with similar interests. It was all very serious and earnest. They experimented with ouija boards and automatic writing. Mrs. John Curran, who made nationwide news with her séances, in which she communicated with the spirit of Patience Worth, lived right down the street and was a great friend. Hadley remained skeptical about it all, even though Mrs. Curran prophesied great things for her future.

As Hadley emerged into adolescence she began to lose the spontaneity and easy gaiety she had had as a child. The atmosphere at home was serious and high minded, and there was little room for fun. Her mother thought that too great an interest in one's appearance was a waste of time, and she considered clothes only from a practical, utilitarian viewpoint. Hadley was never encouraged to experiment with her clothes or her hair, as all her friends were doing. Fonnie did not seem to have been affected by this, but Hadley felt awkward and insecure about her appearance and continued all her life to imagine that she had no clothes sense at all.

People who came to the house were primarily friends of Mrs. Richardson. She allowed no liquor to be served, not even a glass of sherry, and the evenings would be given over to serious philosophic, social, and religious discussions. More and more Hadley found she did not agree with her mother's ideas, nor could she share her interests. She resisted her mother's constant authoritarian direction and began increasingly to shut herself away from her domineering influence. Hadley's ready wit and warm responsiveness were locked further and further below the surface. Although Fonnie had some of her mother's desire to dominate, Hadley had none at all. But she was stubborn and determined not to let her mother rule her. The result was predictable—intense conflicts in which Mrs. Richardson, far stronger, succeeded in blocking her daughter at every turn.

Perhaps as a result of Hadley's childhood accident, Mrs. Richardson decided that her daughter was extremely fragile physically. Hadley occasionally had fainting spells, and her mother succeeded in persuading her that she was not strong enough to do many of the things she wanted. That was the whip with which she forced Hadley's unwilling submission.

Hadley longed for contact with friends who spoke her same inner language, where she could really be herself, but she did not know where or how to achieve such contact. She was searching for something but she did not know what it was. She knew only that she wanted a very different way of life than she had to live at home. And she was not willing to compromise.

At the dancing club, The Fortnightly, she was shy and unsure of herself, a far cry from her childhood when she had so easily entered into everything. But she was critical there too and was going through what she remembers as her "terrific fit of sincerity," a period when she would refuse to make any effort with people unless she really liked them. Needless to say she was hardly a success at these dances.

It was in music that Hadley began to find a release for her intense inner life for which she had no outlet either at home or anywhere else. She had advanced steadily her playing, and though her English teachers at school thought she had a talent for writing and encouraged her to work more at that, she stuck determinedly to her piano. She performed at the music club and at various benefits and even had a studio recital of her own. She began to dream of a career as a pianist.

The summer that Hadley was seventeen, Mrs. Richardson took her two daughters for a European tour. Having spent so many years abroad later in life, Hadley remembers very little of that first trip—the terrible heat in Italy where she fainted several times; the mosquito which got under the netting of her bed in Florence; and the persistent headaches which finally alerted her mother to the fact that she had puffed up her hair by wearing a "rat" in it, something Mrs. Richardson had expressly forbidden. At each stop the first visit was to the American Express, where Fonnie would rush to pick up mail from her beau, Roland Usher.

On the boat going over they met a remarkable couple, Otto Simon and his wife Anne. Mrs. Simon was a gifted pianist and teacher and took a great interest in Hadley's music. She proposed that Hadley should leave school and come and stay with her in Washington where she would train the girl as a musician. More than ten years later Hadley could remember her disappointment when the plan did not succeed. "How I wanted to do it," she later wrote. "About that age the charm of academic work was breaking and I began to feel all sorts of things that met no understanding much in school and to be very bored. . . . And this Anne Simon loved music, had every kind of genius and sympathy for it—and a very thorough technical ground besides— and thought I could do anything . . . I do know I was malleable and sensitive enough to learn awfully high things. . . . Then because it was considered foolish to take me out of school before graduating, it all fell through. I was bitterly disappointed and came back to the dusty, prosaic school rooms and American jokes and stupid school-girl stuff." [2]

Hadley was nineteen when she graduated from the Mary Institute in 1910, having lost a year along the way due to illness, and Fonnie married Roland Usher in June of the same year. He was later to become an outstanding historian and professor of history at Washington University in St. Louis. Mrs. Richardson turned over the ground floor of the Cates Avenue house to the young couple, and she and Hadley had a separate apartment upstairs.

Hadley's musical ambition had waned temporarily, and although she remembered that Mrs. Simon had thought college would be wrong for her, she was determined to go to Bryn Mawr where one of her friends from the Mary Institute was planning to go. In order to satisfy the Bryn Mawr requirements she had to take a test in German, so the summer after her graduation from school she tutored in that language and passed the examination successfully.

Bryn Mawr was a great change from the quiet life on Cates Avenue with her mother and sister. Hadley's room in Pemble West was filled night after night until past midnight with girls full of intense ideas, and animated discussions took place about life and purpose and ideals. Hadley could not help laughing a little at the high seriousness of it all and nicknamed the group, "At Home to the Infinite." Although she enjoyed it all very much, she found it exhausting.

She would occasionally visit her father's sister, Aunt Mary Rosengarten, who lived on Rittenhouse Square in Philadelphia. Aunt Mary was active in all sorts of philanthropies and was president of the St. Cecilia Society. She was another forceful character who wanted to "do over" Hadley, change her clothes, the way she did her hair, and so on. But Hadley did not want to be directed by Aunt Mary any more than by her mother and managed to stand her off. But she did enjoy Uncle Frank Rosengarten, who liked to laugh as much as she did and invariably referred to Fonnie and Hadley as Finnan Haddie.

Hadley stayed only one year at Bryn Mawr. Physiology was

her nemesis, and she remembers having received a 27 on the final examination. There had been just too many people, too much to do and talk about and experience. Not only did her academic work suffer but her health did too. More than ever Mrs. Richardson was convinced that Hadley was not strong enough to live anything except a sheltered life, and that she must avoid all strenuous exertion and over-excitement.

A tragic event which occurred the summer after she left Bryn Mawr was to have a lasting effect on Hadley's next years. It was Hadley who answered the phone at Annisquam and was given the news that her sister Dorothea had been in an accident. A brush fire had broken out near her house and in her attempt to help put out the blaze, her kimono had caught fire and she had been terribly burned. A few days later she died of her injuries, after having given birth to a stillborn child. Hadley remembers going numb at the news. Dorothea had been the one person she could always count on.

With the end of her college plans and her return home, Hadley took up her music again, this time more seriously than ever. She had not changed at all in her desire to find something more in life than a conventional home, a conventional husband and a predictable future. She later described her view at that time of marriage as a "trap. I used to rant and rage [to] myself—no one need expect *me* etc." [3] Through music, if she could make a career of it—and she was determined to do so—she could escape all traps. She was ready, as she later wrote, to "throw over everything for it—people, parties, beaux, because I couldn't combine them with it." [4]

She found an interesting new teacher. Harrison Williams was a young pianist who had studied abroad with Godowski and Busoni, and Hadley learned a great deal from him. He was a perfectionist and demanded professional standards from her, which had a good influence on her from a technical point of

view, but tended to inhibit the expressive aspects of her playing.
It was natural enough that she fell in love with Harrison Williams. He represented everything that she cared for at that time.
But although he was very fond of Hadley and they remained
friends for many years, he did not reciprocate the degree and
intensity of her feelings for him.

It took Hadley several years to get over this attachment, years
in which her hopes of a musical career were also disappointed.
She simply did not have the physical strength and stamina for it.
It was a long time before she could admit to herself that "I de-
teriorate physically beyond a certain amount of work—just about
the amount that marks the beginning of genuine achievement." [5]
She tried very hard to ration her forces. One year she would rest
fifteen minutes for every half hour at the piano. She later described how she was "sure at first that my body would stand it,
then beginning to fear, then gradually giving in, then for fear of
unhappiness trying to throw it over altogether, then not being
able to endure it, starting over again—too violently." In the end,
although all her life she would love to play the piano, she gave
it up as a serious ambition "in favor of health and balance." [6]

Hadley did not know what she wanted to do with her life
after that. The family relationship at home was much too close.
Hadley more than ever came under the pressures and direction of
her mother. She did not agree with any of her mother's ideas nor
did she share any of her interests. Mrs. Richardson and Fonnie
got along extremely well together and the two of them were full
of ideas about what Hadley should do and think and be. Hadley
quite naturally resented this, but it was not easy to stand up
against a person as strong-willed as her mother. The result was
that Hadley withdrew more and more into herself. During her
three years of working intensively at the piano she had isolated
herself and had lost touch with her frends. She was nearly
twenty-four years old and felt now that she had no objective in

life. It was constantly being impressed on her that her health was extremely precarious, that she could not do this, or should not do that. Living as they did in such close proximity, with Fonnie right downstairs, Mrs. Richardson and Fonnie formed a strong team. There was no place for Hadley to go. Whenever she would suggest the possibility of travel or somehow getting away from home, she was made to feel that she "was an invalid and shouldn't even spend a night alone." [7]

These were difficult years for Hadley, lightened only by her friendship with the George Blackman family. There she found a congenial atmosphere and the kind of people with whom she could feel at home. She looked forward every week to their Sunday evening open house. Young poets and painters and a few professors from the university attended regularly. There was always an open discussion in which everybody took part, sitting in a large circle, some people on chairs, others on cushions on the floor. Mr. Blackman knew how to draw out people and skillfully guided the conversation into interesting channels. Hadley enjoyed those evenings but she was far too shy to enter into any of the discussions. Even at the Blackmans, where she felt at home, she was unable to break through the wall she had built around herself.

One of the Blackman daughters, Elsa, sought Hadley out. Hadley felt no constraint at all alone with Elsa and would pour out her feelings and thoughts. Elsa undoubtedly filled to some extent the void left by Dorothea's death. There was Elsa's brother, too. Occasionally he would take Hadley to a dance and assure her that she was not at all the fright she thought she was and that with smarter clothes and more attention to her appearance she would be extraordinarily attractive.

Hadley felt she would never have managed those years without the Blackmans. "I couldn't have lived, literally, without them," she wrote later. "I'd have become an onlooker only they unconsciously ship you on to fight and grapple with things." [8]

When the Blackmans moved to California, Hadley's only congenial contact was gone. Resisting as she did the pressures of her mother and sister, believing that her health was indeed precarious, she let life slip by her, only venting her feelings at the piano. She knew there were all kinds of wonderful things going on all around her, but for a long time she took almost no part in any of them.

Even the war years more or less passed her by, although she did do some work at the local library, sorting books that had been donated for the servicemen. She still longed to get away from home, but every time she mentioned it there would be a scene which broke even more any confidence she might have had that she could live an independent life. Her brother-in-law, Roland Usher, sympathized with her and hoped that she would get out and go abroad, and Hadley sympathized with him for being a part of this intensely female household.

It was only when Hadley was twenty-eight that the long period of seclusion began very slowly to end. She started seeing some of her old school friends again and meeting young men and going out to parties of people her own age. She was still very shy and unsure of herself but she gradually began to realize not only that people liked her and found her attractive but that they enjoyed her sense of humor and that she could make them laugh. Tall and slender, with long, thick, shiny red hair, she was a striking figure who drew attention in any group.

She took up tennis and was surprised to find that she was good at it. This encouraged her to realize that she was not at all as fragile physically as she had been led to believe.

Her mother did not completely approve of all this and was especially wary of the young men who paid any attention to Hadley. Mrs. Richardson was an ardent feminist and suspicious of men in general, but especially of any who might engage Hadley's interest. One evening when a new beau came to call on Hadley, her mother sat with them in the living room the whole time, imposing such a frost that he never came back again.

There was one beau, however, of whom Mrs. Richardson thoroughly approved. He was Dr. Leo Loeb, a brilliant scientist, one of the great pioneers in the field of cancer research. He was more than twenty years older than Hadley, and would come to call most decorously, engaging her in serious conversation and urging her to read books on science. But Hadley did not respond. She enjoyed her younger friends far more.

Hadley's life changed suddenly in the fall of 1920, soon after her tenuous re-entrance into the world had begun. Mrs. Richardson died after an illness of several months, during which Hadley devoted herself to caring for her. When it was over, Hadley was physically and emotionally exhausted.

Hadley was finally free from the dominating influence of her mother, and it would be many years before she would realize what a remarkable woman in many ways Mrs. Richardson had been. But after her mother's death, Hadley had even less of an idea what she would do with her life. She had been sheltered for so long she did not know where or how to begin. She would still have the apartment at Cates Avenue where her sister and brother-in-law and their four small children lived downstairs. Hadley could not envision her life beyond the narrow confines of being a maiden aunt to the children and an occasional companion and help to her sister. She scarcely ever touched the piano any more and she sometimes wondered if she would ever be able to play again. She enjoyed seeing her friends and going to parties, but something was missing. She still wanted a deeper meaning to her life, but her feelings were vague and undirected and she did not know exactly what she did want or how she could set about finding it. Although she had plenty of beaux now, there were none who really attracted her. As she later wrote, "not a soul hit my soul's centre all summer long." [9] Nearly twenty-nine, Hadley was almost resigned to spinsterhood.

When she received a letter from her old school friend, Kate Smith, inviting her to come to Chicago for a good long visit, Hadley was delighted. Kate wrote that she herself was living at the Arts Club, but that Hadley could stay with her brother, Y. K. Smith and his wife, Doodles, at their apartment. It was October when Hadley set off for Chicago. For years she had been "starved for people [who] really might mean something" to her.[10] After her Chicago visit that would never be true again.

CHAPTER

II

HADLEY FELT immediately at home with Y. K. Smith and his wife. It had been a long time since she had been with people she found so congenial. Kate scarcely gave Hadley time to unpack and settle in before she announced that she had invited a whole group of friends over for the evening. Hadley put on her new dress for the occasion, navy blue and beautifully tailored. Kate tried to explain to her who was coming to the party, in addition to the four young men who were living at the Smiths'. Nevertheless, Hadley was overwhelmed with all the people who burst into the apartment, laughing at everything, using a kind of glib private language mixed up with pig Latin, and calling each other by a strange assortment of names. It was impossible to keep them all straight: Horney Bill, Boid, Little Fever, and one in particular who stood out in the hurly burly and who seemed to have the largest assortment of names: Oinbones, Wemedge, Nesto and others of which she could not begin to keep track. It was some time before she learned his real name: Ernest Hemingway. Hadley was soon given a nickname of her own: *Hashadad* which was quickly shortened to Hash.

She later described for Ernest her first impressions of him as "a pair of very red cheeks and very brown eyes straddling the piano bench while Bill wrote down statistics (all wrong) that Katie and I gave as to the population in China and other foreign parts. You surprised me I remember by seeming to appreciate me without my succeeding, from excitement, in doing anything to be appreciated. I tho't he likes me because my hair's red and my skirt's a good length but wait till he hears that I'm a player of classical music and do not care for Harold Bell Wright." [1]

Ernest did more than appreciate her at that first meeting. He decided that she was the girl he was going to marry. Hadley was flattered by his attentions but she was not at first attracted to him although she believed that most of the other girls were. She recognized an intensity in him, a kind of excitement that heightened everything and everyone around him and she sensed quickly that it was he who took the lead in the group. She thought him very handsome, and even glamorous in his Italian officer's cape, but she felt a more subtle face and temperament would have suited her better. She enjoyed the evening enormously, however, and laughed as she had not laughed in a long time with this fun-loving company who seemed at once to accept her as one of them.

The three weeks that Hadley spent in Chicago were full of excitement, the center of which increasingly grew to be Ernest. She was more and more impressed with him, his vitality, his charm, his drive, his determination to wrest from life what he wanted. In spite of the fact that she was eight years older than he, she felt he had lived and experienced far more than she.

In the spring of 1918, at the age of eighteen, Ernest had volunteered for the American Field Service. His first assignment was as an ambulance driver behind the Austrian front in Italy, but his eagerness to see the war closer at hand caused him to seek front-line canteen duty. He was in the trenches one night, distributing cigarettes and chocolate to the soldiers, when a fragmentation bomb landed, exploding on ground contact and hurling hundreds of metal fragments with tremendous force. Although his legs were streaming with blood, Ernest picked up and carried a wounded comrade, succeeding, he never knew how, in bringing his burden to safety even after he was hit again by machine-gun bullets which tore into his right knee. He spent long months in the hospital after that. It was there that he met Agnes von Kurowsky, one of his nurses, and for the first time fell deeply in love.

When at last, in January 1919, Ernest returned home to Oak Park, Illinois, it was to be acclaimed a hero. For a while it was enough just to be back, to bask in the admiration accorded him, to convalesce, and finally to find his legs strong enough so that he could go off on fishing trips to all the old boyhood places. But eventually all this began to lose interest for him.

He was hurt and bitter when Agnes wrote him that she had fallen in love with someone else. Most of his friends were working or away and his parents began to put pressure on him to do something. After graduating from high school and before going off to war he had worked for six months on the *Kansas City Star*, but he was not ready now to tie himself down to a regular job. What he wanted was to do some serious writing. He spent some time at Petoskey, near the Hemingway summer home in Michigan, but had no luck at all in marketing the stories he wrote there. He stayed for six months in Toronto as a sort of companion for the young son of a wealthy family there and did some writing for the *Toronto Star*.

The summer before he met Hadley had brought things to a climax with his parents. Dr. and Mrs. Hemingway had grown increasingly anxious about Ernest's development, or rather what they thought of as the lack of it. Dr. Hemingway worried about his lack of responsibility. Strong-minded Mrs. Hemingway was even more forthright. He must completely change his ways, his loafing and pleasure seeking, trading on his good looks with girls and spending his money wastefully on luxuries. She made it clear that he must make his own way and that he would not have their approval unless he changed radically. Underneath all his bluster, Ernest was hurt by their attitude and lack of belief in him.

Ernest moved to Chicago only a few weeks before he met Hadley. His old friends Bill and Kate Smith suggested that he could stay with their brother, Y. K., while he was getting settled. There he found his wartime friend Bill Horne. But jobs were not easy to find and money was very short. His only income was from occasional pieces used by the *Toronto Star* and a bit of advertising copy once in a while. The picture was hardly a reassuring one for a proper, conservative young lady from St. Louis who had been brought up with all the correct ideas of what one should look for in a young man. Yet Hadley was impressed with Ernest's confidence in himself. He seemed to her to know absolutely what he wanted to do and to have complete faith that he was going to do it. She did not at first feel this same "glorious faith in his future," but she soon learned to be sure of it too.[2] As soon as she returned to St. Louis, Ernest began bombarding her with letters.

Life at home was very different now than when Mrs. Richardson had been alive. Hadley had found two friends to share her apartment, Ruth Bradfield and Bertha Doan. They entertained a great deal, went out to parties together, and for the first time since the Blackman family had moved away from St. Louis, Hadley had someone with whom she could freely exchange confidences. She expanded in this easy, uncritical atmosphere. It was like a long delayed coming out, and Hadley thrived on it. She had a great deal of lost time to make up for, and though she was still shy and not yet completely sure of herself, she had all the friends and admirers any young woman could want. And every day, in untidy envelopes that had a "clutched-in-the-hand, stuffed-in-the-pocket look," came long letters from Ernest.[3]

At first Hadley answered decorously once a week, not believing that this young man was really as serious about her as he claimed. And his bitter experience with Agnes raised questions in his mind too. "What do you mean," she wrote him on New Year's Day 1921, "you want me to go on loving you a little while at least? Don't you expect to hold out very long yourself, Nesto? . . . Do you mean at all that you don't feel the capacity to stand the long strain of things and circumstances on our companionship?" She hoped not, she told him, but now was the time to say it if that was how he felt.[4] His reassurances drew from her the response, "Yes I do too know how much you love me." [5]

Very soon, however, her own feelings were completely engaged too. She felt he was a perfect companion because he was "so generously loving," and she wondered if everybody knew "how very lovely a person you are." She loved his spirit, she told him, and was proud and appreciative of his mind "even up to where I have to get off and wave an affectionate farewell." She was vastly impressed with the "beyondness of his work and—oh a sort of grasp on large things—judgement and stuff," which she felt she lacked.[6] Hadley felt strongly her inexperience and lack of knowledge of life and she sensed a maturity in Ernest which she respected and looked up to.

Nevertheless, the eight-year difference in their ages (at that time Hadley thought it only seven) concerned them both, although in different ways. Ernest was determined that it made no difference at all, and yet it was a subject that had to be settled between them. "Ernest, *I* have never taken an attitude of olderness to your youngerness in anything that mattered, have I?" Hadley wrote him. "Good Lord knows I don't feel that way, honey. Don't see how I could. Seems to me you're a wise man and much much beyond me in experience and understanding . . . I can learn from you every minute of the time and then some." [7] Nevertheless, she thought often how nice it would be for him to have someone like herself, only younger. "But you're tired of

having that thought occur to me, aren't you?" she told him.[8]
For him the whole subject finally became "taboo" and eventually she agreed with him. "You don't think *I* give a damn about ages, do you? Only I had to honestly give you a look in on maybe its making a difference." She has always had friends herself of all ages, she tells him, but she wanted to be sure he "didn't mind it. Course if you weren't maturer than that it *would* be wrong." It would be terrible if she felt the capacity to lead him around.[9]

Ernest had finally found a job in December 1920, with a monthly magazine in Chicago, *The Cooperative Commonwealth*, where he served in many capacities—as writer, editor, investigative reporter, on one occasion writing practically the entire issue himself. It was hard and demanding work and took most of his time and energy away from his own writing. He looked on it as a mere stopgap and he was full of all sorts of different ideas and plans for the future.

He had been homesick for Italy almost from the time he had left and when a wartime friend returned there and suggested Ernest come along, his imagination soared. When he wrote Hadley about getting married in the fall and going together to Italy her "reaction was so great it oughtn't to be put down." But the same day she received another letter from him talking about the possibility of his becoming editor-in-chief of a weekly magazine. "These letters require answers," Hadley wrote him in some confusion. "The one about Italy is *so* exciting and the one about *Barchetti's Weekly* so excited—I can't tell which is what nor why . . . I can't tell whether you want to . . . stick around in America or make the bold penniless dash for Wopland." What she is most interested in is to do what will be best for his work. "I really value your ambition so much," she tells him, "I couldn't help you to throw it aside even for a short while to hasten the good time. I want to be your helper—not your hinderer—

wouldn't for anything have your ambitions any different and admire 'em so. So anything you suggest that means putting the work in secondary place has no backing from me." Italy might possibly be the solution to everything, she thinks.[10]

Ernest was obviously torn between his desire to go abroad, cutting all dreary job ties and concentrating on his writing, and the obligation he felt to accumulate some capital toward what he should be able to offer a wife. "Me, I don't need to worry about all these things your darling heart suggests," Hadley encouraged him. "I tho't going to Italy on the much less money nescessarily cut out the worry of having to wait around and make hoards and piles instead of working and living along in the same way we want and people should—with the person they love —and seeing peachy people and having brain work and some out-of-doors and stimulating people and environment." She believes that there will always be ways and means of doing good things and leading a good life, and is sure that they both know how to do it without much money or ideal surroundings. "I'm not at all the woman [who] wants her practical future guaranteed," she assured him.[11]

Hadley was living in a busy round of activity and gaiety. She had started playing the piano again and was practicing hard— Ravel, Rachmaninoff, Albéniz, Bach, all the things she used to love. She wrote Ernest how thrilled she was about it. "Think if maybe I could play again!" [12] she exulted. She was asked to play at the Wednesday Club and was as active as she could be, ice-skating, walking, visiting art galleries and concerts, dinners, lunches, dances, busy with something every day. The girls bought a Victrola and moved the furniture around in the living room so that they could dance, and all their friends were contributing records for it. Hadley was especially fond of Murad cigarettes, and cocktails and highballs were served regularly.

Ernest too was seeing his friends, going to the theater when he could afford it, boxing whenever he got the chance, and working hard, especially at the end of the month when the magazine was put to bed.

In spite of all the plans and hopes that flew back and forth between St. Louis and Chicago, nothing definite had been settled yet about the future. Hadley and Ernest had discussed marriage, but so far only in vague terms. After all, they had seen each other only during a brief three-week period and needed to be together again even though the daily letters were a continuous chain between them. Ernest kept hoping he could get down to St. Louis, perhaps with Kate Smith who wanted to visit her aunt there, but money was very low and he could not afford the trip.

It was early in March 1921 before he was finally able to come, after several changes in plans which left Hadley and Kate's aunt "cussing you and Kate, keeping us waiting round and wondering when you'll descend." [13] But three special deliveries arrived in one day with definite news of his arrival. "Great great joy and delight and pleasure and gayety all mixed up in me at once . . . Everything else is blown aside and nothing matters." [14]

It was a fine visit even though Hadley felt somewhat shy and not able to express her feelings as she would have liked. They both agreed that a weekend was much too short a time to be together after such a long separation and so it was planned that Hadley would go to Chicago as soon as possible.

Hadley's sister Fonnie raised the question of the possible impropriety of such a visit under the cirmumstances. Although Fonnie told Hadley she liked Ernest "awfully" and found him "well-behaved," actually she had not been impressed with Ernest and felt he was not the kind of man whom Mrs. Richardson would have approved. Hadley, nevertheless, was determined to go to Chicago and managed to resolve the whole situation to Fonnie's liking. So off she went, most properly chaperoned by her friends Ruth Bradfield and Helen and George Breaker, only a few days after Ernest had left.

Ernest and his friends gave them all an excellent time. He took Hadley out to Oak Park to meet his family and she found "they all, specially Mrs. Hemingway, were perfectly wonderful" to her.[15] She sensed that they considered it was a "great thing for Ernest to marry this sedate little St. Louis girl," as she later described it, but she thought that they were worried for fear that Ernest would "do something that would not be really helpful to a sedate little bride." [16] Hadley, however, had complete trust and confidence in Ernest and she knew that what he needed more than anything was someone to love him and believe in him.

They went out with Kate Smith and Bill Horne, and Hadley wore her handsome black satin dress with Bulgarian embroidery. One evening, when they were all at Y. K. Smith's apartment listening to a recording of Rimsky-Korsakoff's *Scheherazade*, Ernest pulled Hadley over beside him on the sofa and announced, posing majestically, that they were the prince and princess. Hadley was embarrassed nearly to tears by this childish display and was appalled at Ernest's enjoyment of it. Later they argued. Ernest said he would like to be a king. Hadley could think of nothing less appealing, and the words flew. "But he probably would have made an awfully good king," she said later.[17]

"No one was ever sweeter to anybody than you are to me," Hadley wrote him after she got back to St. Louis, "straight through everything in every way. You know I'd love you even if you weren't so gentle and darling but I can't tell you how complete that quality makes my loving. Thank you for everything that made me have such a wonderful time in Chicago—and Allah be praised that we are living at the same time and know each other." [18]

Hadley was excited that Ernest had seemed to be simply "busting with material" for writing "and square in the middle of a creative *mood* too." [19] Soon afterward he wrote her about a "novel busting loose" in his brain. "Why I don't believe and never have for a long time that dull periods with you mean a thing but creation going on inside," she told him. He evidently had certain doubts about his ability yet to write a novel and was fearful it might be considered too youthful. "Juvenilia! Pooh," Hadley wrote him. "Thank the Lord, some young one's gonna write something young and beautiful. Someone with the clean muscular freshness of young things right on him at the moment of writing. You go ahead. I'm wild over the idea, Ernest—and the *start!* That's the way for a novel to start, with real people talking and saying what they really think. . . . I'm *all for it* and so violently for *you* as a person and a writer and a lover I can't put it down on this paper." [20]

Ernest had begun saving money for Italy and buying lire to take advantage of the exchange rate. Hadley was worried that he was not eating enough or properly and "you didn't honestly try boxing to make us seeds?" she asks worriedly,[21] using Ernest's jargon for money. They had discussed her own small inheritance and she thought it was "jolly for us both about my sweet little packet of seeds from my banking grandfather, James R." [22] This was a trust fund which might be counted on to bring in a couple of thousand a year.

As usual, Ernest continued full of different kinds of plans of what he wanted to do. No fixed date had yet been set for the wedding but that it would take place sometime in the autumn was clear. He wrote Hadley about the possibility of moving to Toronto where he could work for the *Toronto Star*. Hadley was as enthusiastic about that as about any of his ideas. He suggested that if she got lonely up there she could always come home for a visit and said he did not think separations were bad. Hadley agreed that it is often sensible and healthy for people to separate for a while. She had reached the conclusion that "if you love someone very much, know definitely that it's someone you're going to care about permanently . . . then the way to show it is to give that feeling the tenderest, loving attention and care, watch to see what it needs, like a child or a garden—and be doing something for it all the time." She did not mean constantly hovering, that would be insufferable, but just letting "the sun and the rain and the will of the gods have their play." [23]

In spite of their brave talk about separations, they were both feeling the effects of this present one. "Aren't we both funny lately?" Hadley comments. "So low and droopy and not able to stop missing each other a few minutes and whisk a good time out of somebody else." [24] Ernest had completely broken through the wall that she had maintained around herself for so many years, and she trusted him absolutely. For her, he was a "most healing and wonder-person." Being near him "removes every fear and worry." [25] She loves the fine clean quality in him that runs clear through. "I never expected to find anyone into whose life I could fling my spirit—and now I can—every side of me backs you up," she told him.[26]

Ernest felt that Hadley was "an artist," and to some extent she agreed. She believed that she was "too near at being one to be happy without some little bit of subtle presence of beauty but too far to be productive." And she found it a "rather lacerative sort of person to be." [27] She had long since forgotten any regrets about her abortive efforts towards a musical career, nor did she feel the years she had struggled were wasted. "It was meant to be that way," she told Ernest. "As it is I'm awfully happy because I'll amount to a thousand times more with you and also I've got a lot of stuff that you like in me, maybe even need in me, just simply because I did hang on so many years and tho't and tho't of that one art." [28] She recognized that "a few years back we couldn't have married and been happy because I couldn't have used my best forces for you—just loving you. Ambition as well as passion for music, would have kept me unhappy because married I think I could never satisfy either. Reason is I love you and have conquered all but the worshipping side of my feeling for music." [29]

Ernest's letters kept pouring in, one, two, and sometimes three times a day, and even the postman became intrigued with the whole affair. Hadley realized more and more how important to Ernest her interest in his writing was, and she thought he even sometimes sounded scared about it. "I've no volition in the matter," she hastened to reassure him, "I *am* interested—I'm right *in* it . . . Your writing is of vital interest to me, personal and impersonal . . . I've never been terribly fond of anyone [who] hadn't had some such contact with intangible things as you have. But you're honestly the first one that's ever satisfied me as having the capacity to go the whole wonderful circle, intellectually and spiritually. Course you have miles to go and wonderful miles they'll be and you're panting to be off and definitely laboring towards an end, aren't you? Think of me being with you and not from objective knowledge but from having the same nature in my own way, being happy over all the new material of technique and insight and viewpoint that will rush to the open channel you are." [30]

In spite of all the other possibilities that Ernest was exploring, the escape to Italy remained their prime goal. He continued to economize in every possible way and Hadley sent him some money with which to buy lire and add to his store of them, which she told him he could repay to her gradually if he wanted. She hoped they wouldn't fail in their Italian plan. "Think of how in Italy there won't be anything but love and peace to form a background for writing," she told him, "and what with all this seething writhing mass of turbulent creation going on inside of you now and busting loose now and again in spite of lack of ideal opportunity—why you'll write like a great wonderful sea breeze bringing strong *whiffs* from all sorts of strange interior places, you know. It's hard as the dickens to wait for but it's fun to be working for it." [31]

Ernest managed to come again to St. Louis for a visit over Memorial Day with his friend Bill Horne. Ernest stayed at the apartment with Hadley, properly chaperoned by the two friends living with her, and she was happy to "have this place full of you at last." They again had a very gay time with parties and visits and an all-day excursion and picnic on the Meramec River.

Many years later Hadley remembered doing something that day at the river which she thought "quite wicked" of herself. Some time earlier Ernest had given her a beaded bag. It was beautiful, wide and deep, of a lovely sea green color. The only trouble was that it was not quite new, and here and there beads were missing. Ernest was always a bargain hunter, she said later, and she thought this kind of gift was characteristic of him. But she was annoyed about the missing beads and felt it would be impossible to find matching ones and have it properly mended. When Ernest took her out in a canoe on the river, she let the bag slip from her grasp and it disappeared in the water. She thought he was sad about the loss but that he was not quite sure whether she had done it by accident or on purpose. Neither of them ever mentioned it and fortunately it did nothing to spoil their happiness at being together.[32]

Bill Horne enjoyed Ruth Bradfield and called her B.L.G. for Beautiful Little Girl, and Hadley expanded happily with Ernest in the feeling of security that "you're the most completely encircling warmth and light and love about me."

Nevertheless, Hadley was still a little shy and quiet in Ernest's company and envied him his freedom and ease with people. "I haven't *anything* to say to a soul," she complained. "Funny how wherever we go together you seem to have thousands of things to say to everybody—I stand back and admire because I can't do it myself any more—maybe get it back sometime? Used to be very enormous talker—wouldn't know it now, would you?" [33]

The wedding plans began to crystallize and although a firm date was not set during the visit, they discussed where and how they wanted to be married. Ernest called it "the act of spliceage" and Hadley referred to it as "all this September stuff."

Mrs. Hemingway had written Hadley suggesting Windemere Cottage, the Hemingway summer home on Walloon Lake in Michigan, for the honeymoon. There was a little church only a few miles away at Horton Bay, a small settlement consisting of a few houses, a post office, and a general store. From early childhood, Ernest had loved the place and was great friends with Liz Dilworth and her family, who ran a famous chicken dinner place there called Pinehurst Cottage. Hadley's friend Kate Smith, and her brothers, Bill and Y. K., had spent many summers there with their aunt, Mrs. Charles, who had taken over the care of the children after their parents' death. "Auntie" was a great friend to Hadley too. It seemed a place where they could have the kind of simple wedding that they both wanted and Hadley was doing her best to ensure. "This wedding business has so painfully little connection with marriage," she told Ernest, "that I'm going to suffer pushing kind friends and family off of fuss and stuff . . . I *shake* with fright and being a *spectacle* while the whole point of loving you is the main thing and that's been going on for a long time." [34] The one thing that she wanted to avoid was having the wedding in St. Louis where it would be impossible to evade her sister Fonnie's arranging things according to her ideas.

Fonnie, however, was far from reconciled to the idea of Hadley marrying Ernest. She dragged up again the question of Hadley's physical fragility with which Mrs. Richardson had so long undermined Hadley's confidence in herself. She claimed that Hadley was not well enough or strong enough to marry or to have children, and Hadley was horrified to learn that she had even discussed all this with Ernest during his visit. Hadley was furious at this unwarranted invasion into her intimate, personal affairs and faced her sister with it. They had a scene, and Hadley told Fonnie once and for all that it was none of her business. But with Ernest just as angry about it as she, and her roommates equally outraged and understanding, she did not fall into the old feeling of helpless depression from which she had suffered in the past when she had tried alone to stand up against her mother and Fonnie. Now, although it did remind her of that long period when she had felt "as tho' I were ground right down to a root of myself," she could shrug it off as she had never been able to do before because she had, at last, gained some confidence in herself and, as she told Ernest, "we believe in each other—and what can *that* do to *us*." [35]

Some of Ernest's friends thought "marriage a peculiarly unfitting state" for him, and Hadley felt it took a good bit of courage on her part to stick on in spite of their reservations. But she was "just as sure as sure that we're meant to be happy, to enjoy work to be done—and I hope we never lead the hand-rule scheduled life most people do." [36]

For years she had wanted to break out of the strict conventionality in which she had been brought up, and she was determined not to let domestic trivia or pressures of conformity constrain her and Ernest. "It would be frightful," she wrote him "for a person like you, that is so wonderful, so everchanging—whose big value is a great resounding reaction to every sort of thing—to be afraid some one he loved very much was going, consciously or not, to level him down to smooth even feelings and tho't. I would break up anything rather than do that." She is sure that she herself will "*never* tie down tight to domesticity and just *stick* there." If she feels this way about herself, how must she feel about him who she knows "to be very much more highly charged with life in every form." [37]

III

Ernest was not able to get down for the party that Hadley's friends, Helen and George Breaker, gave on June 14, 1921, to announce the engagement. There were only thirty people, "all people who would care," but Hadley felt her "heart pounding like mad" at the prospects of making it all public. At a recent gathering, she found herself saying that Ernest was the first American *killed* in Italy. "They haven't stopped laughing at me yet," she told him.[1] The newspaper spelled her mother's maiden name wrong, Ernest's name "Hemmingway" and mistakenly wrote that he had attended the University of Padue, but Hadley did not mind.

Hadley and Fonnie were "friendly again." Hadley believed Fonnie would not interfere any more and she was glad "the miserable homesick feeling of being off good terms with my only family is gone."[2] In spite of the friction between them and Hadley's resentment of Fonnie's efforts to direct her, there was a real attachment between the two sisters.

Hadley was busy choosing her wedding dress, with three or four friends "hanging breathlessly over each curve." It is a creamy lace, the loveliest thing she ever imagined and makes her look "like a human hazelnut tart," she tells Ernest.[3] She is

buying all sorts of pretty things for her trousseau and is busy
sewing and altering and getting everything in order. She de-
scribes everything in detail to Ernest and obviously is taking a
greater interest in her clothes than ever before.

In spite of so much to do and all the happy anticipation, both
Hadley and Ernest found it no easier to be apart, and they were
often depressed. When Hadley was told by one of her friends
that the engagement period is the best time, she disagreed thoroughly. "It seems to me everything lovely and wonderful is to
come," she wrote Ernest, "sort of like the difference between
studying the sun thru astronomical methods and simply and joy-
ously living in a country saturated with sunlight." [4]

The tension of the long separation continued to build, and
Ernest was even more depressed than Hadley. He was not happy
at his job, he had a bad sore throat and Hadley was distressed
that he found "time so harassing and not getting you anywhere
at the office." He even began to doubt her feelings for him. "So
you tho't I was off of you? Entirely? Oh Oin!" she answered. [5]

In addition some of his friends continued to voice their doubts
about his marriage, which Ernest passed on to Hadley. She
finally reacted forcibly. The first thing she had heard, she told
him, when she returned from Chicago when she first met him
was that "the whole Charles family, including Bill [Smith] had
told Fonnie you weren't estimating yourself low enough, from
the point of view of literature, considering the way you were
not working." She thinks if his friends have "an ounce of the
logic men are supposed to have" they ought to be glad that
"some sort of thing to get you going a little bit . . . comes along
and loves you and chimes in with you. We're PARTNERS,
Ernest, and if this here heart-busted bunch think there's anything fatal to the success of our plans in that they really ought
to SAY what it is . . . No use saying I'm the perfect woman for
you—might be an enormous, healthy mistake. I'm sure I don't

know. God hasn't told me a single secret about it. Just the same I think in the same way He hasn't told them a thing either . . . And if I hadn't been aware of my ability to back my single self financially well enough at any time, I wouldn't have let you, ever, take me on." She loves him very much but does not see why he throws all these vague hostilities at her. At least he should explain his own reactions. All she asks is to be able to face the situation squarely.[6]

Before that letter reached him Hadley received one from him which shook her badly. Ernest's depression had not lightened and he even mentioned suicide. "What's this?" she answers him. "Not truly so low as to crave mortage, are you?" And she tells him "the meanest thing I can say to you on that point is to re-member it would kill me to all intents and purposes . . . You *gotta* live—first for you and then for my happiness." She tried to encourage him but realized that she could do little at such a distance. "You mustn't feel so horribly un-worthy, dear Oin," she told him. "It's because you *are* sick—what you should do is give way physically . . . Your description of your end of our engagement is ghastly. Glad you wrote it out—I knew it was hard . . . Think we might both feel a little happier if we could see each other right now, do you? That's why I hope it will be decided for me to come up now, unless it would entangle the work too badly."[7] Five days later she went to Chicago for the weekend. All the tensions were relaxed, and both of them felt much revived after her visit.

When Hadley returned home she felt "so well and gay . . . awfully up to snuff." She had loved everything about the trip, she wrote him—the people she met, Kate's dancing, the white wine, but best of all "was every once in a while finding your old eyes, gleaming and warming and softening at me across the table."[8] And she was vastly relieved to hear "you're sounding so well again and on top."[9]

Hadley was occupied with parties, arrangements, seeing friends, trying to pack her books and "tons of music" to be ready to be sent to her when she will want it. Ernest planned that they would live at Y. K. Smith's apartment and Hadley thought "our little room . . . will be terribly adorable." [10]

Mrs. Hemingway had been pressing Hadley for some time to fix the exact date of the wedding "but the ways of the Lord are uncertain and even He doesn't know," Hadley tells Ernest, but adds that she will answer soon. She wrote Mrs. Hemingway that "the date of the wedding has to be slightly elastic until a few more questions are settled, but I'm sure it's going to be the first week in September." [11] It was finally set for September 3, 1921, at four in the afternoon. Hadley asked for the name of the church to be put on the wedding invitation. Wedding lists began to crystallize and quickly reached four hundred and fifty, "but we're in a tremendously cutting mood and may get it smaller yet," Hadley tells Ernest.[12] Hadley had hoped her brother Jamie could give her away, but he was not well and would be unable even to attend the wedding. Fonnie would be there, however, and Hadley's close friend, Ruth Bradfield, and of course Kate Smith and the Breakers.

Much more important than all this was Ernest's twenty-second birthday and the things he had been writing. Hadley gave him a Corona typewriter with her "most tremendous tender and admiring love." [13] She was "absolutely wild" about a poem he sent her about the Corona and simply "worships" another poem he called "Desire."

> And all the sweet pulsing aches
> And gentle hurtings that were you.[14]

His two-page satirical story, "A Divine Gesture," left her breathless. "It's the most wonderfully keen and superbly done thing!" she wrote him. ". . . I'm completely under its power. Cynical—yes—but as fine as the finest chain mail." [15]

Hadley planned to go with her friends Helen and George Breaker for the final weeks before the wedding to a lake in Wisconsin, stopping en route for a visit with Ernest in Chicago. "Combined with letters to be written, trunks to be hauled down and packed, music, books, investments, thanks, etc. I know full well I cannot leave here Wednesday next—but I shall anyway," she writes him. "And it's all so joyous," she adds, "and so sad." Hadley found it sometimes a "terrible heartache" saying good-bye to some of her friends, but she was "weeping, starving lonely" for Ernest.[16]

All her sorrow at parting, however, was dispelled as soon as she saw Ernest. "Oh I had the most heavenly time," Hadley wrote him the day after she left Chicago for Wisconsin. "I had such wonderful hours with you, on the roof—nights of mist and fireworks and nights of quiet stars and feverish city lighted 'scrapers' around—and hours in the office when I could watch this strangely impersonal man moving about . . . Wonderful times of hand-in-arm breathing—together, stepping together thru streets alive with personalities that almost never reached 'my quick' . . . on account of being so selfishly, deliciously engulfed in your companionship." [17] When she felt Chicago, Hadley was so excited that she forgot her umbrella at Y. K. Smith's apartment, her jewelry in the safe at the hotel, and Ruth's bridesmaid's hat in the stateroom in the train, and spent a good part of the morning tracking down all these objects.

She was staying in a log cabin on a lake near State Line, Wisconsin, where she planned to spend the month of August. She found it hard to settle down after all the excitement and activity and tells Ernest that she and her friend Helen Breaker, "aren't as you might say, possibly, in tune with the infinite quite yet. Still, we'll taste and smell the water and wind and pines again and that's enough to make me happy." But, "How I wish that you were here!" she adds.[18]

The weather was cold, especially after the heat of St. Louis, and Hadley came down with a bad case of tonsilitis. Ernest too had a sore throat again. He was busy looking for an apartment for them to live in, as the plan of staying at Y. K. Smith's had fallen through because of increasing personal tensions between them. Hadley worked hard on budgets—$75 a month for rent; $90 for housekeeping, which included such items as $6 for milk, $30 for meat and vegetables, $2 for eggs and so on, plus $69 for his lunches and miscellaneous expenses and the hope of managing to save to buy more lire. Hadley worried whether she would recover her health before the wedding, but the doctor reassured her.[19]

Through all the confusion of wedding lists, budgets, plans for the honeymoon, and so on, Ernest's work was still their primary interest. He was continuing with his ideas for a novel and wrote Hadley of the problems he faced with it. "It'll be *wonderful* to have you writing a novel," she answered him. "I'll be as happy as happy to be with you thru it all or be kicked out or slid into a corner or anything you like . . . Yes, I can see how your first novel, that'd cause most terrific throes of all, might be too chaotic—lose itself—that isn't always so." [20] She enclosed the wedding invitation.

Ernest finally found an apartment in Chicago in a made-over house on North Dearborn Street and sent Hadley a plan of it. She was delighted with it and could find everything on the plan "except how a person enters in the first place—must be somewheres between the bathroom and the trick bed, correct? At first it looked as tho' the guest would have to enter thru the bath itself—sort of on the foam of a shower like Venus." It is a furnished apartment but he had not let her know whether there were linen or dishes. "Oin—we *gotta* have dishes," she tells him. If none are available she can arrange to have some sent from St. Louis.[21]

Time began to pass more quickly and soon she wrote him that "two weeks from today we'll be playing together at Walloon Lake with a day and a night behind us and many days and nights ahead of us to love each other in." [22]

Hadley had hoped that since her brother could not come to the wedding to give her away perhaps her uncle, Arthur Wyman, could officiate, but as he too was unable to come it was decided that George Breaker would take over as Jamie's representative. "Auntie" wrote that the organist at Horton Bay can play only "Throw Out the Lifeline" and do they want her to get one from Petoskey. And what about a minister? "Oin," Hadley pleads, "I don't know *one thing* about ministeriats . . . You gotta get the minesterial." [23]

All these were still details, however, compared to what Ernest kept telling her of his fermenting ideas about things he wanted to write. "Oin, I'm treading on air about these novels!" she tells him. "It's the greatest news ever, and it's really criminal we aren't free yet to put your best time and thought in them. But there'll be spurts now and *later*—in Wappa—our lives will be so vital on account of that thing in you that flares out and has to be set down." [24]

Ernest arrived at Horton Bay a few days before the wedding and set off at once with two of his friends to the Sturgeon River for the fishing he had been dreaming of so hard all summer. Hadley arrived September 2, the day before the wedding, and she and her sister and the three girls, Ruth Bradfield, Kate Smith, and Helen Breaker stayed with Kate's aunt, Mrs. Charles. Hadley felt it was hospitality itself and she was not nearly as nervous in anticipation of the ceremony as she had expected. Mrs. Charles gave her "several warning cries" about Ernest, that he would be difficult and so on, but Hadley rendered "such an impassioned description" of what he was like that Mrs. Charles finally said, "If he's like that, he's ideal." [25]

The day of the wedding was perfect. The little church was decorated with wild flowers which Ruth and Kate had arranged. Ernest went for a swim before dressing for the ceremony and so did Hadley, but it took longer for her thick hair to dry and she was late at the church. Her creamy lace dress was as becoming as she had hoped it would be, and she radiated happiness as she came down the aisle on George Breaker's arm to the strains of the wedding march played by an organist imported from Petoskey. Dr. and Mrs. Hemingway were there with two of their daughters, Ursula and Carol, and their six-year-old son, Leicester. Hadley had her sister and her closest friends as attendants, and Ernest was supported by five of his group, with Bill Horne as best man. There was a little of the young men's customary ribaldry with some of them announcing outside the church, "Kid Hemingway now going to the mat." Ernest managed to step on Hadley's white slipper as they came out of the church, and the indelible mark it left pleased her. He was irritated at all the picture taking afterward, but they all had a good chicken dinner later at Liz Dilworth's Pinehurst Cottage. It was dark before Hadley and Ernest managed to get away. A friend of Ernest's drove them over to Walloon Lake where they climbed into a rowboat and rowed across to Windemere Cottage.

Weeks before the wedding Ernest had written Hadley worrying about how they were going to get their meals on the honeymoon. She had been quite confident that it would work out very well except that she might be so much in love with him that she would not do her bit very cleverly at first. But she found it difficult to keep house in this large family cottage of the Hemingways that seemed to her to stretch out all along the shore of the lake. She couldn't find anything—pots, pans, salt, kettles, or pepper. And they both had bad colds. The weather had turned cooler but there was an open fire, and they had a hot brew going into which they kept pouring liquor.

Ernest took Hadley into Petoskey once and introduced her to several girls he had known in the past. Hadley did not enjoy that at all. She thought it was his form of braggadocio and although he tried later to appease her by saying that he thought it would raise him in her estimation to show her these girls "who cannot live without me," she found his explanation hardly satisfactory.[26]

They went one day to lunch with Ernest's mother who had a cottage of her own across the lake. Hadley did not feel any rapport with her and she could understand how it was that the relationship between mother and son was strained. Nevertheless, she made every effort to be attentive and affectionate to her mother-in-law. A letter of welcome to Windemere Cottage that Mrs. Hemingway had wanted Hadley to have had been lost, and Hadley learned of its existence only after the luncheon party. She wrote Mrs. Hemingway immediately to apologize for what she feared would impress the older woman as "my apparent ingratitude for your welcome and your explanation of many material comforts." She and Ernest were "terribly sad to be leaving Sunday for we have had a most heavenly time here together," she added. "We've enjoyed everything—the great fire and eating in the cozy old kitchen after the wind of autumn began to rumple things up too much to take our meals in the open air dining-room." [27]

After a two-week honeymoon they moved into the little third floor apartment that Ernest had rented at 1239 North Dearborn Street in Chicago.[28] It was unattractive and depressing, in a poor section, and Hadley felt somewhat lost in the big city especially as Ernest was out most of the day. Her best friend was the groceryman around the corner. "He could talk," she remembered long afterward, "and he could smell a lonely woman." [29] The apartment was so small they could do almost no entertaining, but they did go out in the evenings a good deal with the old gang, although Ernest and Y. K. had quarreled and broken up completely.

Mrs. Hemingway called on Hadley one day soon after their arrival with the pious idea of instructing her about "love." Not sex, of course, which was an unmentionable topic, but Hadley felt the older woman wanted to make sure that her son had a real love. Since Hadley was aware of the long-standing, bitter friction between mother and son, she hardly responded favorably to this well-meant but tactless intrusion. In revenge, when they attended a big evening party at Oak Park to celebrate Dr. and Mrs. Hemingway's wedding anniversary, Hadley perversely did not wear any of her pretty clothes, although she knew all the other women would be elaborately dressed. Shortly afterward, when she and Ernest and one of his boxing friends were invited to a public fireman's ball, she put on her most elegant dress and was the belle of the party.

All their plans for budgeting their money, the lists of expenses and economies they could make in order to save for their trip to Italy were shattered when Ernest resigned from his job on *The Cooperative Commonwealth*. He had been increasingly aware that something was seriously wrong there, and he did not want to be involved in the predicted bankruptcy. He still wrote occasional pieces for the *Toronto Star*, but their only assured income was from Hadley's small trust fund. At that point their prospects for going to Europe looked hopeless, but everything changed suddenly when Hadley's Uncle Arthur Wyman died, leaving her a completely unexpected inheritance of eight thousand dollars. With this windfall that seemed like a fortune to them, they began at once making plans to go abroad.

The previous spring, through Y. K. Smith, Ernest had met Sherwood Anderson, whose work he greatly admired. Anderson had interested himself in the younger man and on one occasion had evidently compared his writing to that of Kipling. When

Ernest reported this to Hadley, she was not impressed. "As to comparing you and Kipling," she wrote him, "that's foolish cause Heavens—why I don't want to compare you to anybody. You're Ernest Hemingway and doing your best—it's not like anyone else's best or worst at all." [30]

Sherwood Anderson and his wife Tennessee had spent the summer in Europe. Shortly after their return they invited Ernest and Hadley to dinner. Anderson told them that although the *dolce vita* in Italy had its appeal, the real place for a writer to go was to Paris. That was where the really serious work was being done. He spoke glowingly of the life there, the interest they would find, the favorable rate of exchange. It was not difficult to persuade Ernest and Hadley.

By the end of November their plans were complete. Ernest would write free-lance articles from Europe for the *Toronto Star*. Anderson advised them where to stay in Paris and wrote letters of introduction for them to Gertrude Stein, Sylvia Beach, Ezra Pound, and Lewis Galantière, wonderfully praiseful letters about this very young and as yet untried writer which would assure him of entree into the literary colony of Paris. In early December, when Hadley and Ernest boarded the train for New York, they felt their life together had really begun at last.

CHAPTER

IV

THEY SAILED December 8, 1921, on an ugly old boat, the *Leopoldina*. Ernest was jubilant, in one of his moods of roistering gaiety. Hadley was a little put out that several of the girls on the boat seemed always to be around. She felt inexperienced with these chic, clever young things who flirted with Ernest, and though he seemed unaware that they had any special interest in him, Hadley was not sure of her ability to compete. Although Hadley had thought that she and Ernest would be "all in all to each other," she soon saw that Ernest drew people to him wherever he went. But Ernest was in love with her, and she with him, and they felt right and secure together.[1]

At Vigo, where the boat stopped briefly, they had their first view together of Spain. They walked arm in arm together through the cobblestoned streets and along the wharves, where Ernest began Hadley's education in fishing lore, pointing out of her the huge tuna which he said were the kings of all fish.

Paris was wet and cold when they arrived there just a few days before Christmas. Sherwood Anderson had recommended the inexpensive, small Hotel Jacob, on the rue Jacob off the rue Bonaparte. It was clean but very simple and Hadley recalls the holes in the staircase carpet which Ernest referred to as "traps for drunken guests." The hotel was bursting with Americans, hopeful artists and writers, and a good many pseudo-aspirant types too, but it was good to have Americans about, especially when you were a little frightened of the strange city and very homesick.[2]

Hadley was fascinated by the rue Bonaparte, the street along which Balzac, Victor Hugo, Georg Sand, and scores of others had passed on their way to the offices of *La Revue des Deux-Mondes*. The rue Visconti was forbidding, its narrowness emphasized by faceless buildings that had long ago housed resolute Calvinists. That most ancient part of Paris, the Ile de la Cité, with Notre Dame, the Sainte-Chapelle, and its long sense of the past, was only a short walk from the Hotel Jacob. But Hadley and Ernest were eager for the reality of the present, for the teeming, pulsing life of the people of that "marvelous strange city, marvelous and awful." [3]

Paris with Ernest was exciting, but it was Hadley's first Christmas away from home, and much as they tried to hide it from each other they were homesick. With their limited finances they never took taxis and did not yet know how to manage the buses. Besides, they both loved to walk. They started off Christmas morning strolling down the rue Bonaparte, along the Seine and across it, and the length of the Avenue de l'Opéra. By that time they had worked up an appetite. There was the Café de la Paix. They examined it judiciously and decided it looked the kind of place that would suit both the occasion and their limited budget. They had aperitifs and a fine meal that cheered them up even though it was unlike any Christmas dinner they had been accustomed to. Then the bill arrived. Later Hadley could not understand how they had missed adding up the prices of what they had ordered, but there it was. And they did not have enough money with them to pay the total. Ernest left a very nervous Hadley alone in the restaurant while he returned to the hotel for more money, running as fast as he could both ways. She was terrified the whole time he was gone for fear he would be hit by a car or that something would happen to prevent him coming back for her. When he finally did arrive they paid the bill and left the restaurant at once. Neither of them felt like celebrating any more, and none of it was anything like home.[4]

One of the first people they met was Lewis Galantière, a friend of Sherwood Anderson's, who invited them to dinner at the fine Restaurant Michaud, which was a treat as usually they had their meals at a small café around the corner from the hotel, on the rue des Saints-Pères frequented by students from the medical school nearby. Galantière was erudite in everything French and knew Paris well. A man of exquisite tastes, his apartment was filled with choice objects which he liked to show off, and he was an ardent collector of fine engravings. He put Hadley immediately at her ease and she thoroughly enjoyed his tart wit. Towards the end of dinner Ernest brought up the subject of boxing and, as soon as he learned that Galantière knew something of the sport, insisted on taking him back to their two small rooms at the hotel for a few rounds of sparring. Galantière agreed reluctantly. He did not like to box and never could decide which he disliked more—hitting or getting hit. Although Hadley had worried a good deal about how she would react when she saw Ernest box, and perhaps get hurt, she had soon become case-hardened. She had even acted as his second, more for show than anything, when he organized an exhibition match on the *Leopoldina* for the benefit of a Frenchwoman and her baby, deserted by an American husband and returning to France. On this occasion in Paris, however, there was no question of Ernest being hurt for he outweighed and outreached Galantière massively. The two men put on their gloves and began circling and feinting. The whole procedure struck Galantière as more and more absurd and after a minute or two, during which not a blow had been struck, he laughed and said it was enough. Drawing off his right glove he tucked it under his arm, picked up his glasses from the table and began removing his left glove. Ernest continued to shadow box, bobbing and weaving about. Suddenly he struck out, full in Galantière's face, breaking his glasses. Almost miraculously neither Galantière's eyes nor face were cut. Ernest, although hardly contrite, seemed relieved that Galantière had escaped what might have been a serious injury.[5]

It was Galantière who helped them find an apartment that would suit their needs and more especially their budget. The apartment they chose was an oddly shaped two-room affair on the fourth floor of an old building at 74, rue du Cardinal Lemoine. At every landing on the spiral staircase was a faucet and the ubiquitous French *pissoir*. The apartment was all funny angles and corners, and the furniture was "very elegant." In the bedroom was a great, gilt-trimmed fake mahogany bed, but the mattress was good, as it would be in France. The dining room was crowded with an ugly oak table and chairs. Both rooms served some of the functions of a living room. The bathroom consisted of a recessed closet with pitcher, bowl, and slop jar. Only one person at a time could get into the kitchen, with its two-burner gas stove. Slop jars had to be emptied at the landings and the garbage carried down the long four flights. The only heat was from a fireplace in the bedroom where they burned coal *boulets*.[6] The other tenants were simple people, rough but kindly, all "salt of the earth with a little dark dirt mixed in." [7] This was a poor working-class neighborhood.

Next door to number 74 was a dance hall, a Bal Musette frequented by sailors and workingmen, a ten-cents-a-dance kind of place where you bought tokens for dances from the sharp-eyed manager. The slow shuffling of feet and the sound of the accordion were clearly audible in the Hemingways' apartment upstairs, playing them to sleep and often waking them up during the night.

Just down the street was the Place de la Contrescarpe, where the dregs from the rue Mouffetard would congregate in noisy bistros. Years earlier the *Place* had been the site of the celebrated Café de la Pomme de Pin where Villon and Rabelais used to visit, and Racine and La Fontaine, perhaps even Descartes, who had lived not far away on the rue Rollin. This part of old Paris, and especially the rue Mouffetard, was far off the beaten tourist track, a place where you could see life as it was lived by the majority of poor Parisians; where housewives searched for bargains in food, not for fancy French cuisine but for subsistence; where one could see tired beggars hoping for alms in front of the ancient church of Saint-Médard, much as Victor Hugo had described it when Jean Valjean recognized among the beggars the sharp eyes of Inspector of Police Javert; where drunkards lay supine in doorways, undisturbed by the heavy tread and hoarse singing of coal merchants hauling endless sacks of *boulets* up narrow staircases; and where at night people tried to forget the harshness of their lives in raucous gaiety.

The Hemingways were hardly settled in their apartment when in January they went off for two weeks in Switzerland. They chose a small village named Chamby, above Montreux, where two of the pretty girls from the boat were also vacationing. The Hemingway finances were just as tight as ever, but they traveled third class on the train and the Pension Gangwisch was very reasonable. Hadley had already noticed that they always managed to have money for the things they really wanted to do, and so they outfitted themselves with all the necessary equipment and started to learn to ski. Hadley liked the sport immediately, learning at first much more quickly than Ernest whose leg, still stiff from his war wound, made it more difficult for him. Later he surpassed her. After the busy weeks in Paris, the clear air, the stillness, and the beauty of the Swiss mountains were refreshing. They both missed their friends from home, but they had each other and a whole world of things to explore and experience, and there was never anyone who was better company than Ernest.

They came back to Paris "both of us in the pink of condition," Hadley wrote to Mrs. Hemingway. Hadley was "delighted with discovering the possibilities of our apartment. It certainly *is* crowded," she admitted, "but it is undoubtedly comfortable. I have my piano in what was the dining room (a brand new Gaveau upright) and the dining table is in the bedroom and is used as a work and writing as well as a meal table." She wanted the girls to know about the Paris fashions, skirts were long and so were sleeves but "the best looking hair here is invariably bobbed." [8]

The weather had cleared, and it was dry, sunny and very cold, and the city was lovely. Ernest, however, was out a great deal, darkness came early, and the streets were filled with strangers. Hadley, with her vivid red hair and her American clothes, which she felt the French were fascinated by but did not approve of, was ill at ease alone in the rough neighborhood of the Place de la Contrescarpe. She had heard much about Frenchmen and "thought they were all terrible devils." [9] Her school French— and she had been an excellent pupil in it—was hardly a preparation for the language as it is spoken in Paris, especially far from the regions of the Grands Boulevards. It took her a long time before she found she could cope with the swift argot and familiar coarseness of the rue Mouffetard.

Ernest had no such reservations, however. Hadley believed that he was a person who had the gift of being at home anywhere, that not only did he have tremendous courage but the confidence of making "a good and stalwart impression, of arousing respect and interest and admiration." [10] He was fascinated with their neighborhood, and Hadley wrote that he was "deeply engrossed in Hilaire Belloc's *Paris* [which] tells such a lot about this old quarter built by the *Romans*." [11]

He read all the French sports magazines and though his accent was execrable, he quickly learned to communicate without any inhibitions about grammar. He used to walk a great deal through the city, dressed simply in cap and worn jacket, looking like "a real son of the people," and Hadley thought that helped make friends for him.[12] He liked the simple people of Paris, the taxi drivers, the shopkeepers, the bartenders, the jockeys, the boxers, the ones he felt really knew what life was all about. If there was anything that Hemingway hated it was pretentiousness, and the French people have an unusual gift for deflating pomposity.

Ernest's writing was the focal center around which everything revolved. It was the reason for their move to Paris, where they hoped that Ernest would escape the pressures and harassments, the limitations and shackling of his spirit that he had felt at home. They could live economically, with Hadley's little nest egg and modest income, and Ernest would be free to write as he wanted. He rented a small room on the rue Mouffetard, in the hotel where Paul Verlaine had died. Here he spent long hours every day working to perfect his style, experimenting endlessly, searching for the ultimate in distiliation and clarity.

Ernest was strict about his working hours. He and Hadley would have breakfast together, "but please, without speaking," and then he would be off to work in his room on the rue Mouffetard. Sometimes, when the work didn't go, he would trudge through the streets of Paris, observing, absorbing impressions and then go back again to wrestle at the Corona that Hadley had given him. She remembered that often when he came home after a long day there might be just one single line that he "could hang onto without hurting his conscience, his terriffic artistic conscience." [13] But Hadley never doubted that he would succeed in what he was striving to achieve in his work.

Hadley did not mind the morning silence. It was a good silence, and Ernest needed it. She thought that Ernest's friends imagined that life with him must be a constant ferment of fun and gaiety, not realizing his need to be alone, to gather into himself with total concentration. Hadley too liked to be alone sometimes, but she recognized that for Ernest it was essential and she never felt that he was neglecting her, although some of her friends tried to persuade her that he was.

The woman from whom they had rented the apartment put them on to Marie Rohrbach, a Breton peasant woman always known by her familiar nickname of Marie Cocotte. She came every day between four and eight in the afteroon, "cleans a bit, fills the pitchers, fixes the grate fire, washes the breakfast dishes, washes or irons a little and gets a delicious meal," Hadley wrote her mother-in-law.[14] Marie Cocotte took an immediate and avid interest in the young couple. She taught Hadley how to run a small ménage in Paris, and gave her the first lessons in French cooking. It was when Ernest was finished with his work for the day, however, that Paris really came alive for Hadley.

Ernest was hesitant to follow up the letters of introduction that Sherwood Anderson had written for him, eager and yet a little shy to meet these famous people, and somewhat on the defensive when he finally did go. Hadley remembers their first visit to Ezra Pound's studio on the rue Notre Dame des Champs, a great big ugly room with a shelf running all around it, stacked high. Ernest listened quietly while Pound talked and drank what seemed to Hadley at least seventeen cups of tea. She thought Dorothy Pound a lovely person and liked Ezra and was pleased at his interest in Ernest's writing. Soon Ezra was visiting them regularly at their small apartment. Hadley was proud of Pound's interest in Ernest's work and his efforts to help the young writer.

"Ezra Pound sent a number of Ernest's poems to Thayer, of the 'Dial,' " she reported to Mrs. Hemingway, "and has taken a little prose thing of his for the 'Little Review,' also asked him to write a series of articles for the 'Dial' on American magazines." Although in the end they were rejected, Hadley felt that "it is all surely most flattering." [15]

They did not know just what to expect when they called on Gertrude Stein. A very correct maid in white apron and cap answered the door and ushered them in, through the small foyer, to a wonderfully long, comparatively narrow room. Alice Toklas came forward to greet them, looking, Hadley remembered, like a "little piece of electric wire, small and fine and very Spanish looking, very dark, with piercing dark eyes." Way over at the far end in the corner by the fireplace sat Gertrude Stein, a figure like the great god Buddha, as Ernest used to say. Hadley though her head and face "absolutely beautiful," with the most wonderful eyes she had ever seen, beautiful brown eyes that saw everything. She was small but heavy, with enormous breasts, which intrigued Ernest and he wondered how much each one weighed. "I think about ten pounds, don't you, Hadley?" he asked.

Hadley had looked forward to meeting Gertrude, who at once beckoned Ernest to a chair near her while Hadley found herself on the other side of the room, having been deftly removed by Alice Toklas. Hadley discovered later that many other wives had had the same experience and she felt that Alice Toklas instantly took firm charge of wives unless the wife happened to be a famous writer. She engaged Hadley in animated conversation, asking her all sorts of questions about current affairs of which Hadley knew nothing. When she discovered Hadley's ignorance, she proceeded at length to enlighten her. Hadley, however, would have preferred to sit and listen to what Ernest and Gertrude Stein were discussing but that was not allowed there.[16]

One of the focal points in their lives was Shakespeare & Co., the bookstore and library run by Sylvia Beach. She let Ernest borrow as many books as he wanted and keep them for as long as he liked. He was a voracious reader, and though Hadley tried, she could never keep up with the rate at which he devoured books, magazines, newspapers—everything in print. He was ready to read anytime, any place. Sometimes when he had his arms around her and she would snuggle down against his shoulder, she would suddenly sense something, turn her head and find that he was reading a folded-up newspaper held behind her back.

Sylvia Beach knew all the most talented young Americans and French of the literary world and was generous in including Ernest and Hadley among her friends. Through Sylvia they met James Joyce, whom Ernest admired, but he was not a readily available friend, and the Joyce family kept themselves aloof.

What Hadley missed most was the warm companionship and easy camaraderie of the girls she had seen so much of during the last two years in St. Louis. Brides are notoriously lonely the first year or so of marriage, but Hadley was especially so, torn out of context, as it were, in a strange city, and with Ernest absorbed and away, busy with his work so much of every day. But Hadley was accustomed to being lonely, and in Paris she felt none of the isolation of spirit which had so oppressed her during her difficult years at home. When she and Ernest were together everything was warm and lovely and she was, after all, as deeply interested in and excited about his work as he was.

Ernest swept her into all his variegated, multifarious interests with that contagious enthusiasm of his which heightened all experiences. Hadley had never seen a boxing match or a horse race. There had never been any hurly-burly at home, no going to see the fights, no roughnecks, none of these "terrific, very masculine sports" to which Ernest introduced her. Hadley "bled with the victims and wept and so on," [17] but she loved boxing, and she thought Ernest most complimentary when he told her she had a back exactly like that of the popular French fighter, Criqui. Ernest would explain to her all the fine points of the sport, keeping up a running commentary at the fights, shadowboxing all over the apartment, illustrating defense and offense and technique until the whole sport came alive for her, not as a brutal spectacle but in all its aspects. Ernest did not want her to miss any of it.

She adored the horse races: catching the crowded bus out to the track, just barely sometimes being able to hang on to the outer edge; going first to look over the horses and decide about placing their bets; stretching out on the grass for a picnic lunch, after which Ernest would let her sleep for a while, for she was an inveterate napper; watching the wonderful French crowds and the whole colorful spectacle. Finally there was the excitement of the race and whether they would win or lose the money they could ill afford to lose.

Hadley felt as if in comparison her whole life up to then had been narrow and constricted in every way. At home she had been almost overwhelmed by admonitions and cautions, by concerns on the part of her mother and Fonnie that she must be sheltered and protected. Ernest thought all such ideas nonsensical and saw far more deeply into the reality of her nature, eager for life and experience, responsive to all sorts of things and people. Hadley was sure that Fonnie did not understand or approve of the way she and Ernest lived, and undoubtedly thought it all very rough and uncouth. But as far as her own feelings were concerned, Hadley believed her young husband knew much better what she needed than anyone had ever done. With his confidence and his enveloping warmth towards her, he plunged her into the fullness of an extraordinarily vital world.

Hadley Hemingway in Paris, 1929

Elizabeth Hadley Richardson at five years

Hadley as a little girl

Hadley photographed in St. Louis

Hadley as a young lady

Uncomfortable in a new hat

Hadley in 1918, two years before she met Ernest Hemingway

Family wedding picture: left to right, Carol, Ursula, Hadley, Ernest, Mrs. Hemingway, Leicester, and Dr. Hemingway, September 3, 1921

The bridegroom with friends and ushers

Ernest and Hadley in the Black Forest, Germany, August 1922

LEFT: Hadley and Ernest at Chamby

Hadley with fishing rods

Left to right: Sally Bird, Ernest and Hadley in the Black Forest

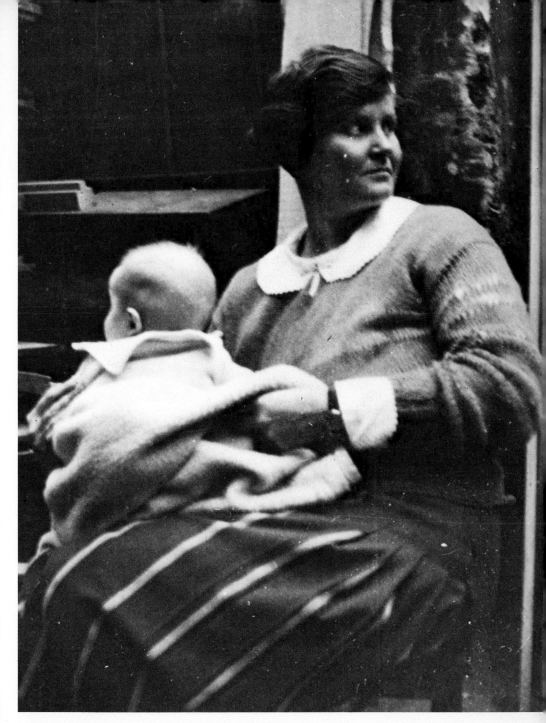

Hadley with her son, John Hadley Nicanor Hemingway (Bumby), at 113 rue Notre Dame des Champs, Paris, spring 1924

Ernest with Bumby, Paris, c. 1925

BELOW: Bumby

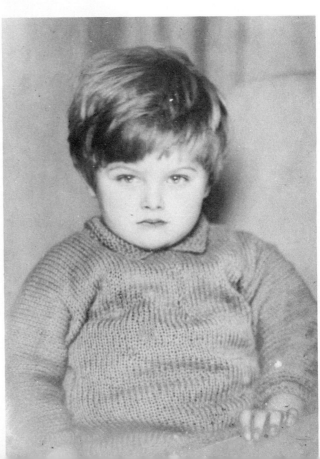

The Hotel Taube,
Schruns, Austria

BELOW: Ernest, Bumby,
and Hadley at Schruns,
1926

Bumby and Hadley at Cap
d'Antibes, France

From left: Gerald and Sara Murphy, Pauline Pfeiffer, Ernest and Hadley (with bootblacks in foreground), Pamplona, in July 1926

Ernest photographed after his divorce from Hadley

Paul Scott Mowrer as a young man

BELOW: Hadley and Paul, February 14, 1958

Hadley and Paul, Canal Point, Florida, March, 1970 (John Penida: *The Miami Herald*)

CHAPTER

V

Eᴿɴᴇꜱᴛ ʜᴀᴅ ʙᴇᴇɴ sending articles to the *Toronto Star* on a wide variety of subjects from tuna fishing in Vigo to hotels in Switzerland, and American Bohemians in Paris. In April he was asked to cover the economic conference in Genoa. He met there a lot of foreign correspondents, including Paul Scott Mowrer, chief of the Paris bureau of the *Chicago Daily News,* who, because Ernest had no arrangements for cable credit, allowed him to charge the dispatches he sent off to the *Toronto Star.* Hadley was lonely and a little frightened without Ernest. There was compensation, however, when Ernest returned with the word that the fifteen articles he had sent from Genoa would give them enough extra money for another visit to Chamby in May and then a trip to Italy where he wanted to show Hadley all the places he had been during the war.

Ernest persuaded his Irish wartime friend, Eric Edward Dorman-Smith, familiarly known as Chink, to meet them at Chamby. Hadley and Chink liked each other from the start, and they all three had a good time, skiing, climbing, talking, reading, and drinking plenty of dark beer. Hadley was more and more impressed with Chink as she got to know him better, with his slow earnestness, his integrity, and the wonderful twinkle in his blue eyes. Most of all she liked the way he was with Ernest and she thought his influence one of the best. He talked a great deal with Ernest about his work and what he did and did not like, and why. And Ernest listened. Hadley did not know that it caused any change in Ernest's method of writing, but it did stimulate him. In everything.

It was Chink who arranged their walking trip into Italy. They took the train to Bourg St. Pierre and then started the long climb to the St. Bernard Pass. With no elephants, Hadley pointed out. Chink at once disapproved of Hadley's shoes, which she had worn specially to impress him, good oxfords from Abercrombie & Fitch. They covered over thirty kilometers the first day, the last half through deep snow up to their knees, climbing steadily, and toward the end Hadley began to wish that one of the big St. Bernard dogs would come and carry her the rest of the way. Her shoes were soaked through and by the time they reached the Hospice, her feet were swollen and blistered. She managed to get the shoes off and her feet into a pair of bedroom slippers. She washed up, put on dry clothes, and ran a comb through her hair, and then, never having seen a monastery before, she decided to explore. She soon came to a place that looked like a long aisle. Starting down it, she was startled when all the twenty-four doors that lined it on either side suddenly opened and from each door a tonsured head appeared. Realizing that probably no woman had set foot there since St. Bernard fathered the place, she backed out as quickly as she could.

They had an uneventful supper of bread and red wine and a substantial soup and were ready to set off early the next morning By then the shoes presented a major problem, and Hadley did not know how she managed to squeeze into them at all. The descent was ghastly, the shoes splitting at the seams and her feet a mass of blisters. Chink would allow them to walk for twenty minutes at a time and then there would be ten minutes rest with feet off the ground. When they finally reached Aosta, Hadley collapsed in bed for two or three days. Even Ernest later admitted that he had had to take a swig of cognac every two hundred yards on the last snowy kilometers of the climb. For a girl who not long before had been considered almost an invalid, this was quite an achievement and had she had proper boots, as Ernest and Chink had, she would probably have come through the adventure unscathed.

She was thoroughly recovered when they reached Milan and they enjoyed themselves, dining out every evening at Campari's or the Cova, Chink and Ernest reminiscing about the war while Hadley listened. They went to the races at the new track at San Siro, where they had great luck, and Hadley, particularly after three cocktails and judicious attention to the racing form, seemed especially successful in picking winners. Ernest interviewed Mussolini and wrote three articles in which he predicted the Fascist take-over of power.

Chink left them at Milan. Ernest wanted to show Hadley the factory which had been the barracks at Schio, the Lago di Garda and Sermione on the quiet point that goes out into the lake, the Piave valley, the riverbank where he had been wounded. But he was bitterly disappointed to find that everything was changed. Never try to go back, he told Bill Horne later, because it's all gone.[1]

After they returned to Paris, all sorts of vacationing friends from home came to see them. One of their amusements, only slightly malicious, was to take some of these visitors dancing at the Bal Musette downstairs. Bates Wyman, one of Hadley's cousins, worked at the Guaranty Trust in Paris. He was something of a snob and he felt sorry for Hadley, "the poor child married to this artistic bum." She resented this, and it was special fun to take him along to the Bal Musette. She would dance with all the sailor boys and anyone else who asked her and make out she was enjoying it thoroughly, even when she was a little frightened at some of the rough types with whom she had to dance, for one did not dare refuse an invitation. And Ernest, in a striped fisherman's shirt, would dance "with anything he could get his hands on." [2]

One of the people Hadley met that summer of 1922 was John Dos Passos, whom Ernest had known briefly during the war. Dos, as they called him, was to become one of her favorites. Much later he married her old friend, Kate Smith.

In August they were off again, this time to the Black Forest for a walking and fishing trip. They flew from Paris to Strasbourg in a small biplane—the first flight for both of them, but they took it like veterans. Hadley, having had to get up at four in the morning in order to catch the plane, dozed the whole time. Ernest had no trouble staying awake.

Hadley had never fished before but she caught three good trout the first time she tried, and Ernest was one of the best teachers to be had. Hadley found she liked to fish, and though she never became a real expert, she was a good enough fisherman to enjoy it thoroughly. Bill Bird, Paris head of International News Service, and his wife Sally, came along too and Lewis Galantière and his fiancée. They walked, and fished, and had picnics on the riverbanks, and at night put up at little inns.

They were back in Paris only a few days before Ernest received word from the *Toronto Star* sending him to Constantinople to cover the war that had broken out in the late summer of 1922 between Greece and Turkey. It had been bad enough, Hadley thought, when he had to leave her to cover the Genoa conference. But Constantinople! That was too far away. Hadley was furious. They had a fearful quarrel that ended with Hadley refusing even to speak to Ernest the last three days before he left. "It was just awful," she recalled later, but Ernest was all she had in Paris then. Although there were other people whom she knew, there was no one to whom she could really talk or with whom she could feel at home. Her feelings after he left were all mixed up with loneliness, guilt at having "lacerated Mr. Hemingway," strong feelings about not wanting ever to stand in the way of his work, and most of all, worry as to whether he would want ever to speak to her again after all the fuss she had made. She should have taken up something to occupy herself, she thought later, but she was in a mood to worry and feel sorry for herself, and the days passed very slowly. She would sometimes walk down and drop in on her cousin at the bank, and his expressions of pity for her made her madder than ever at herself and the whole situation.

Hadley did not reveal her distress to Ernest's mother and wrote glibly how she was "peacefully practising 3 hours a day and gadding about with all the gay people here." She did admit that she missed Ernest "but everyone assures me that he is safe as anything down there and will probably be home soon." His trip had started inauspiciously as he had "sprained his ankle on the way to the train and the taxi driver broke his typewriter." [3]

Ernest was gone three weeks and when he got back he was exhausted and ill and covered with bites and so many lice that he had to have his head shaved. He brought her all sorts of presents, including a wonderful necklace that he had purchased from some of the Russian refugees who were crowding Constantinople at that time and selling their jewels in order to live. It was an enormous yellow amber creation, very old, warm amber, great chunks of it separated by little black beads and ending in a heavy pendant. For her part Hadley found that when Ernest was ill he often felt sorry for himself and she would have to take "great great care of him at those times," which was something she was especially good at it. And so the quarrel was completely forgotten.[4]

In general, they quarreled very little, though both of them

were definitely outspoken and had no inhibitions toward each other. After one of Ernest's periods of self-pity, which Hadley thought he usually thoroughly enjoyed, he would recover and be "on top of the wave, absolutely roistering with the most wonderful joyousness."

Hadley knew that he was sensitive and did not want to show it, and she would notice how his eyes, which she had always found strangely opaque, would turn away with a hurt expression. She felt she occasionally wounded him without meaning to. "I'm unfortnuately a sort of joker," she recalled, "and apt to say something that flashes through my head and out, and often it played hodge with Ernest because he thought it was dead serious." Her impression was that most people thought that Ernest was sure of himself, overly sure. Often he did have the "nerve of a brass monkey," which sometimes embarrassed her. Occasionally he would show a scorn of other people and say exaggerated and outrageous things about them, yet his kindnesses were "just out of this world, just about as far in the other direction." There were times when he meant to be mean, revealing a cruel streak in him. He could explode with anger sometimes, and he did not give up easily on a dislike. Hadley would occasionally try to combat what she thought were some of his unreasonable dislikes. She had little success, however, and did not always have the strength to make the effort. But critical as Ernest often was of other people, and sure of himself as he seemed in so many ways, she felt nevertheless, "in a way he couldn't think ill enough of himself . . . that he had a great inferiority complex which he never revealed." [5]

Something happened that early winter which was traumatic for both of them and which neither of them ever forgot. In November 1922, the *Toronto Star* notified Ernest that they wanted him to cover the Greco-Turkish Peace Conference at Lausanne, and he went off at once in a hurry. There was no

question of Hadley going with him at that time, and besides she
was down with a very bad cold. Ernest kept writing her about a
man he had met there. This was Lincoln Steffens—older, extremely knowledgeable, delightful, and interested in Ernest and
his work. Ernest wanted Hadley to meet Steffens and was sure
she would like him as much as he did. When he eventually wired
her to come down to Lausanne, Hadley thought that Ernest
would like to show Steffens more of his work. So she rounded up
all Ernest's manuscripts and packed them into her little overnight
bag, in which she also put all the necessaries for her train trip.
No one saw her off, as no one knew she was leaving. She reached
the Gare de Lyon well in time for the train. A porter took her
luggage to the compartment, placed her big bag up out of the
way and left the overnight case, with all the manuscripts, where
she could easily get to it. There was still lots of time and so she
went out and walked up and down on the platform where she
met several newspaper correspondents she knew who were going
to the same conference. When she got back to her compartment
she thought at first she was in the wrong one as the overnight
case was nowhere to be seen. But it wasn't in any of the other
compartments either and then she realized that it had been stolen.
She notified the conductor at once and asked advice from some
of the newspapermen aboard. But it was gone and there was
nothing to do. "It was ghastly," she remembered years later,
"perfectly ghastly." She spent a horrible night with "not an
ounce of sleep and so worried about Ernest," wondering how she
could tell him such a terrible thing. He was at the station to meet
her, with Lincoln Steffens. There was nothing to do but confess.
He was very brave about it, she remembered, but she saw that
his heart was broken. Hemingway himself later described Hadley's grief and how she cried and cried and could not tell him at
first. Steffens felt she suffered perhaps even more than Ernest
over the loss. Ernest tried to pretend to her that he might be able

to re-create some of the writing out of his memory "but he
didn't fool me too much," she recalled. And she knew he could
not fool himself about it either. He did not think he could ever
get it again because it had come "fresh from the mint." A lot of
it had been about himself as a young man, and parts of it he did
recapture later to some extent. But what was lost had been so
good, so very good. She never forgot the horror of it.[6] Ernest
rushed off at once to Paris. Perhaps she had not included the
carbons. But they too were gone. He did not tell her, nor did she
ask him what he had done afterwards that night in Paris. He
never told anyone.

Ernest returned to Lausanne in a mood of almost feverish
gaiety. He and Hadley went up to Chamby one Sunday where
"we had three long runs on our old bob [sled], Theodore, or
rather two, then a lovely jam and toast and nut-cake tea at our
own Chalet, seeing the Gangwisches, our hosts of last winter,
then rushed for the train up to Les Avants again and 'bobbed'
down a last time through the most glorious rosy sunset in the
midst of all those snow-covered mountains, swooping down toward the lake." [7]

As soon as the conference was over they moved to Chamby
where they were joined by a whole group of friends including
Chink who came for two weeks over the Christmas holidays.
They went skiing and bobsledding and warmed themselves with
plenty of hot punch in the evenings. Early in January an old
friend of Ernest's from Oak Park, Isabelle Simmons, arrived too.
Hadley found her congenial and she was delighted to have a
female companion for a change. They went together to the hair-
dresser and talked about hairdos; they started knitting sweaters;
they read and discussed a book on Abelard and Héloïse, and
Hadley missed her when she left. She hoped they would see each
other again soon. There was a reason why Hadley was feeling
a particular need for feminine companionship at that period.

During their engagement Hadley and Ernest had discussed how many children they wanted, and where they would be born, but when Ernest learned that Hadley was pregnant, he was shocked. "I'm too young to be a father," he complained to Gertrude Stein, who found it hilarious and repeated it to Hadley. Hadley, of course, was delighted and thought it would be wonderful to have a baby. Ernest tried to adjust to the prospect, though he worried about their financial insecurity and felt the added responsibility would interfere with his freedom to work as he wanted.

Hadley did not curtail any of her activities during her pregnancy. She continued to ski, though she did at least stop trying to do any jumping. Italy had played such a role in their dreams together that Hadley thought it might be pleasant to have a part of her pregnancy there, so from Chamby they went down to Rapallo where they met Ezra and Dorothy Pound and Henry Strater and his wife. They played a lot of tennis at Rapallo. Ernest was as competitive in tennis as in everything else and whenever he missed a shot he would "sizzle." His racquet "would slash to the ground and everyone would simply stand still and cower," Hadley remembered, until he recovered himself with a laugh.[8]

They took a long walking excursion with the Pounds through the hill towns, where Ezra knew everything about each place they visited. They would lunch somewhere on a hillside, fresh Italian bread and figs and wine and sometimes a sausage. Ernest was half in love with exquisite Dorothy Pound, with whom Hadley got along well. Ezra was great fun, more fun perhaps for Ernest than for Hadley, for he had some idea that he and Hadley were "too much alike, both being readheads, in skin and in feelings," and he had rather definite ideas about women's brains, or lack of them.

At the end of the walking tour, the Hemingways went on by

themselves to Cortina d'Ampezzo, in the Dolomites, where they found the skiing still good, though the big tourist season had ended. Ernest had to leave Hadley there for an assignment for the *Toronto Star* in Germany, but she found a stimulating companion who helped pass the time during his absence. Renata Borgatti was not only a great beauty but a first-rate pianist. Hadley finally played for her, very carefully so as to make a good impression, but she saw that Renata, with her Italian temperament, liked a more virtuoso display.[9] They had a good time together, however, talking music and men and marriage.

Ernest came back to pick Hadley up and take her to Paris, where he left her while he went down to Spain with Bill Bird, and Bob McAlmon whom they had met at Rapallo. He returned enthusiastic about bullfighting and suggeested that he and Hadley go for a week to Pamplona for the Fiesta there, which was reputed to draw the finest bulls and greatest matadors from all Spain. When she was carrying the baby, Hadley felt she had at last discovered her true métier, and she was exuberant and more confident than she had ever been. They decided that the trip to Spain would do her no harm and that it would be a great prenatal influence for the baby, which they both were sure would be a boy.

Hadley was as thrilled with Pamplona as Ernest was. He got her up early every morning to watch the bulls run through the town. She loved the crowds in the streets and the singing and tramping and marching and the shrill fifes playing exciting tunes about people and dancing and fighting. The sound of the fifes "just simply made blood-red stripes across your heart," she remembered. And then there were the costumes and the arena and all the majestic symbolism and terrific passions of the fight. Ernest explained it all to her. He was protective when a bull would horn a picador's horse and would tell her to turn away, though she could not help seeing some of the bad part anyway.

She would sit beside him, quietly featherstitching little sacks for the baby, "embroidering in the presence of all that brutality." And wherever they went, Ernest would make friends with the Spaniards, at the hotel, the cafes, and the arena.[10]

When they got back Paris seemed hotter and the apartment more cramped than ever. They were planning soon to leave for Canada, however, as they wanted the baby to be born on that side of the ocean. Ernest was going to work full time for the *Toronto Star*. He felt that he must have a regular income for at least the first year of the baby's existence, but he was hardly excited at the prospect either of a return to fulltime journalism or of fatherhood.

They had been in Europe more than a year and a half when they sailed for Canada, in August 1923, on the Cunard liner *Andania*. It had been a productive time for Ernest. Six of his miniatures had come out in the *Little Review* in the spring of 1923, in the issue which was called *Exiles*. His story, "My Old Man," had been selected for inclusion in *The Best Short Stories of 1923*. He had already received the proofs of his first slim book, *Three Stories and Ten Poems*. Ernest had developed far beyond the satirical story, "A Divine Gesture," about which Hadley had so raved before their marriage. It had finally appeared in a New Orleans magazine, *Double Dealer,* in May of 1922.

Hadley was elated at the progress in Ernest's career. But she was not surprised by it. She had been sure it would come. Ernest and Hadley had arrived in Europe with only hope, determination, and confidence in Ernest's star. He had worked prodigiously, as he wanted to work, and Hadley had loved him and encouraged him and had been "very strict with him too."

Just before they left Paris, Ezra Pound got hold of Hadley. He offered her some advice, and gave her a present. The gift was a "very worn out" brown velvet smoking jacket, which she wore around the house and kept for years. The advice was

rather typical for Ezra. He told her never to try to change her
husband, something with which she agreed heartily, but then
he went on to say that he might just as well say goodbye to her
now, for having a baby would "change her completely. You
just won't be the same again at all." He thought that motherhood
ruined women. But Hadley felt just the reverse. Having a baby
would only give her someone more to love.[11]

CHAPTER

VI

THE HEMINGWAYS found a warm welcome when they reached Toronto, especially from the Connable family, with whom Ernest had lived during his previous stays there. Mr. Connable was the head of the Canadian branch of F. W. Woolworth. John Bone, the managing editor of the *Toronto Star*, was delighted to have Ernest back. Unfortunately, the man who would be Ernest's immediate superior, Harry Hindmarsh, took an instant dislike to Ernest and set out to make things as difficult as possible for him. Hadley was convinced that this dislike was caused by Hindmarsh's jealousy of Ernest's talent and ability.

They found a small apartment overlooking a ravine at the edge of town which they furnished, according to Hadley, mostly with cartons. A lot of their belongings, wedding presents they had left at Oak Park, old things of Ernest's, boxes of Hadley's, things from St. Louis, arrived and the unpacking of everything presented a problem as Hindmarsh kept Ernest occupied. "Ernest is *distracted* by the job which is run on the most crazy uneconomic principles and is also greatly overworked—so many trips, no sleep and countless unimportant assignments." [1] The constant trips began to worry Ernest more and more for he was determined not to be away when the baby arrived. The doctor assured them that the baby would not come until the end of October. Nevertheless, when Ernest was sent to New York early in that month, on an assignment to cover the visit to the United States and Canada of the British Prime Minister, Lloyd George, he left with a feeling of rage and foreboding. He told Hadley that if she needed anything while he was away, she should go and stay with the Connables.

One evening Hadley did feel "too ill to be left alone in the apartment," so she telephoned Mrs. Connable who told her to come right over. They had dinner together and an agreeable time but afterwards Hadley felt an unusual depression which was only increased when Mrs. Connable played all sorts of sentimental pieces to her on the piano. Mrs. Connable soon realized that something was the matter and Hadley finally admitted that perhaps things were starting. Mrs. Connable took charge at once. She got hold of the doctor, hurried Hadley to the hospital, and in less than three hours, in the early morning of October 10, 1923, there was a fine baby boy. Hadley missed Ernest terribly, but she was proud of the easy way she had come through it. Ernest was on the train coming home from Montreal that night. When he arrived at the hospital the next morning straight from the station, he wept from fatigue and strain. He felt that he had let everybody down.

The baby weighed seven pounds, five ounces. He had "big eyes, still blue, set wide apart," Hadley wrote to Isabelle Simmons, "and the most exquisite little ears set well back and close to his head—has lots of dark brown hair too and a large Hemingway nose—stunning build." [2] They named him John Hadley Nicanor. Hadley explained to Ernest's parents that "Baby's third name is the Spanish for Nicholas—Nicanor—not after anyone in particular so much as in memory of our wonderful trip to Spain this summer. *John Hadley* is one of Ernest's pen names and as it includes me, he is really named for us both." [3]

Everything should have been perfect, but their "hearts were heavy," Hadley told Isabelle, "heavy just when we ought to be so happy." Ernest had been "bawled out by that brute at the office for having come to me instead of taking the material to the office himself." She thought they would be leaving Toronto as soon as she was strong enough. "It will kill my Tiny if we stay too long. He is almost crazy." She doesn't see how she can contemplate another big move so soon again, but "staying here is hell." [4] Hadley knew how sensitive Ernest was and this near persecution at the paper was destroying him. "I just can't stand it, Hash," he told her.[5] There seemed to be only one thing that they could do. Ernest must resign from the paper and give up journalism entirely. They estimated that they could manage on Hadley's small inheritance, and they had saved a few hundred dollars from Ernest's salary, which would pay their passage back to Paris. Ernest had worried that having the baby would limit his freedom, that for at least the first year of the baby's life he would have to have a regular job and income. His fears now were proven groundless. As usual, Hadley was ready to accept financial insecurity, this time even greater than before.

Ernest planned to resign from the *Toronto Star* as of January first, and they laid their plans to skip out on the remaining months of their lease on the apartment which they had taken for six months. They were afraid that if they were caught at this it would mean court action, so they arranged to have their things gradually taken out of the apartment by friends. They had an elderly woman to help Hadley with the baby, Mrs. Marchington, who was tall and severe. She noticed nothing of the preparations for departure, fortunately, and the very last weeks they were able to find a younger, more agreeable, woman.

Ernest paid a quick visit to his parents just before Christmas. They were delighted at the change in him, his maturity and his thoughtfulness. Hadley did not accompany him as she was nurs-

ing the baby and was afraid that too much travel would upset
her and him and would interfere with the long voyage and set-
tling in Paris. She was alone Christmas Eve but they made up
for that the next day when Ernest arrived, laden with presents
from his family and played Santa for the baby "who was all joy
to see his parents dancing around." [6]

They sailed from New York on January 19, 1924, aboard the
Antonia, seven months short of the year they had originally
thought they would spend in Toronto. This time they really felt
as though they had broken out of jail and they were only a little
nervous that when the boat stopped at Halifax they would be
caught for defaulting on the lease. Ernest was through with
journalism; they had a fine son whom everybody on shipboard
admired; returning to Paris would be like coming home. And
money? Well, they would manage somewhow on Hadley's
modest income.

The old apartment on the rue du Cardinal Lemoine was too
small for them now, but it was not easy to find anything. Apartments were exceedingly scarce, Hadley wrote Mrs. Hemingway,
and the prices were way up. They found being in a hotel in
one room with the baby, "and all our luggage with all his daily
laundry to do and seeing friends and going out for meals and
hunting apartments a nerve-racking life." They finally found an
apartment that would do at 113, rue Notre Dame des Champs,
not far from Ezra Pound's studio. It was an attractive street in
a far better neighborhood than the old place had been, an easy
walk down the Avenue de l'Observatoire to the Luxembourg
Gardens where Hadley, in good American fashion, could expose
the baby to plenty of fresh air. It was "over a sawmill, or rather
over the house the miller and his wife live in. We have the whole
second story," Hadley recounted, "tiny kitchen, small dining
room, toilet, small bedroom, medium sized sitting room with
stove, dressing room where John Hadley sleeps and the linen and

bath things are kept and a very comfortable bedroom. Way
down and around the corner you are conscious all the time from
7 A.M. to 5 P.M. of a very gentle buzzing noise and always the
smell of fresh cut wood. They make door and window frames.
The yard is full of dogs and workmen." [7] The owner of the sawmill, Pierre Chautard and his wife lived downstairs. Madame
Chautard was a harridan, always complaining and argumenta-
tive. She took an immediate dislike to Hadley and was envious
of the baby, having had none of her own. Nor could she ever
have produced such a fine one in any event, Ernest and Hadley
thought. They both detested her.

One entered the apartment through a long dark hall. On one
side there was a narrow dining room next to a very small
kitchen with the usual two-burner gas stove. Down the hall in
the other direction was a little box-like room which Ernest used
as a workroom. Beyond that was a relatively large bedroom ad-
joining a kind of dressing room in which they put the baby's
crib.

Just down the street on the Boulevard due Montparnasse was
the Closerie des Lilas, a café where Ernest sometimes went to
work in winter, for it was warm and not as noisy as the sawmill
apartment and there were none of the pseudo-artists that Ernest
felt went only to see and be seen at the Rotonde and Dôme
cafés. A lilac bush grew outside on the little terrace where tables
were set up under the trees in fine weather.

Hadley found again her *bonne à tout faire*, Marie Rohrbach,
though they could never think of her as anything but Marie
Cocotte. This sturdy Breton woman fell immediately in love
with the baby and was as proud of him as though he had been
her own.

Ernest and Hadley still invented myriad nicknames for everyone, for the baby, and for each other. Ernest was Tatie, or
Tiny, or Wax Puppy, and Hash was varied with Feather-Kitty,

or Cat. They were always making up little verses for each other, nonsense rhymes some of which Hadley can still remember: "Little wax puppy/ Hanging on the wall/ Won't somebody take me down/ I'm not happy at all." It was all very silly but lots of fun. The baby went through a series of pet names but the one that really lasted was Bumby, which had a nice, solid humming sound to it. Ernest had completely forgotten his feelings of doubt about the baby and showed no jealousy of Hadley's attentions to Bumby. In general Hadley thought Ernest did not have a jealous nature. He enjoyed Bumby thoroughly and proudly reported to his friends each tooth as it appeared.

They played with the baby a great deal, jigging him up and down and singing little songs to him. But you cannot tell a baby, "please don't cry now because I'm writing a book," and it was not easy for Hadley to put the necessary quietus on him during Ernest's working hours. Hadley wheeled Bumby all over Paris in a rickety baby carriage loaned to them by the Straters, while Ernest struggled to write and to keep warm in his little workroom.

Bumby was christened at the St. Luke's Episcopal Chapel with Gertrude Stein, Alice Toklas and Eric Edward Dorman-Smith as godparents, and soon Gertrude added a nickname of her own for him, Goddy. Hadley had them all for a luncheon afterward, and Gertrude Stein remarked that they could entertain kings and queens of all nations with such a marvelous cook as Marie Cocotte.

As the son of a doctor, Ernest felt he knew something about medicine. He believed firmly that a mother should nurse her baby for months and months, and not only was this the best nourishment a baby could have but that nothing more was necessary. Hadley remembered vividly when William Carlos Williams came to visit them and she proudly took him in to see the baby. She had been pleased and flattered when Stella Bowen,

Ford Madox Ford's wife, had said about Bumby not long before: "What a harmonious little face." Hadley repeated this to Williams, who was a medical doctor as well as a poet. He agreed that the face was harmonious, but "Why," he asked, "isn't he wriggling and wiggling and carrying on? What does he get to eat?" Hadley confessed that she was still nursing him at Ernest's insistence, although she herself felt that the supply had dwindled. Williams found the child too pale and too inactive, so he made out a diet that "would have done for Jack the Giant Killer" and almost at once "his cheeks came out like apples, his muscles grew and he was simply aburst with energy." [8]

On the opposite side of the narrow rue Notre Dame des Champs, which was made up primarily of the backs of the shops on the Boulevard du Montparnasse, there was a door that opened onto a flight of stairs by which they could go down and then around and up into a bakery shop and out onto the Boulevard. Ernest knew that Hadley missed having a piano and he discovered that in the basement of the bakery was an old upright that they could rent. Hadley would freeze playing it, but at least she could work her fingers and it meant a great deal to someone who loved music as much as she did.

When they had left Toronto and agreed that Ernest should give up journalism and concentrate only on his own writing, they had known that finances would be difficult and that their only income would come from Hadley's small trust fund. They felt that the trust company that was handling it was too conservative, and when George Breaker, the husband of Hadley's good friend Helen, suggested that if it were turned over to him he could get her a much better income, they thought it was worth making the change. This proved to be a tragic and costly mistake. George Breaker not only managed to cut the capital in half, but Hadley was left without any income at all for several months. Ernest wasted hours and days, writing letters trying to track down all the facts and handling endless correspondence in an effort to salvage what could be salvaged. Hadley felt this a waste of his precious time and was grateful to him for doing it, even though it was as important to him as it was to her. For that was all they had to live on and their bank account was dwindling ominously.

In spite of all their problems, they were happy. Ernest had not yet achieved a major success, but they were confident he was going to. And in the meantime, Hadley knew that he was writing beautifully, creating wonderful short stories. She was at home in Paris now, and they were making new friends all the time. Hadley had gained in self-confidence since she had produced such a handsome child. It didn't matter to her that she had constant sniffles all that winter because she had holes in the soles of her shoes and could not afford to have them resoled, or that she never took taxis anywhere and would often walk long distances to take advantage of cheaper food prices, or that her clothes were worn and simple and out of fashion, a great contrast to those of some of the chic friends they had gotten to know.

People had always been drawn to Ernest, and this became increasingly evident as his personality and talent matured. The Hemingways were constantly enlarging their circle of new friends. Hadley was especially fond of Stella Bowen Ford, liked her paintings, and found her very amusing. Ford Madox Ford was a "great big rosy-faced man with blue eyes, slightly popped." He would go through every meal of the day, she remembered, starting with an aperitif and contining on, having all the courses and all the wines, and liqueurs afterward. One afternoon Stella was doing a portrait of him, and had him propped up on a chair on a sort of dais in her studio, but with all the food and wine he had consumed at lunch he grew very sleepy and finally drooped over, sound asleep, mouth hanging open. Stella caught him just like that. Hadley never knew whether Ford saw the painting, but she did and found it hilarious.[9]

Through Ford they met Harold Loeb and his friend, the beautiful Kitty Cannell. Loeb for a while had edited a small literary magazine in New York called *Broom*. Kitty was fond of Hadley and felt sorry for her. She blamed Ernest for making Hadley live in such a condition of poverty, always "going around dressed in rags," as she thought. Hadley was self-conscious about her clothes but on one occasion when Bill Bird's wife, Sally, had her French dressmaker make a new dress for Hadley, she was embarrassed to tears and refused to accept it.

The Archibald MacLeishes were another couple who joined the new circle of friends. Both Ada MacLeish and Sally Bird had studied singing seriously. Hadley was amused that once their debuts were accomplished they did not pursue their careers any further. Ada MacLeish was extremely chic, with dresses from Paquin and all the great dressmakers of Paris and she sometimes tactfully managed to persuade Hadley to accept some dress she was going to give away.

They all met together constantly, sometimes at each others' apartments, but more often, in French fashion, at cafés and restaurants. The Hemingways went for lunch almost every day to the Nègre de Toulouse, a restaurant where they felt very much at home and they grew to be good friends with all the personnel. Ernest would insist always that Hadley make the salad dressing, which she was sure was no better than what they would have been served, but she would do a lot of measuring with teaspoons and it became quite a ritual.

Ernest found a new sporting interest that year, the six-day bicycle races. They would leave the baby with Marie Cocotte and arrive at the Vélodrome d'Hiver armed with cushions, sandwiches and a thermos of coffee, staying sometimes through the whole night, with Hadley curled up on the bench for naps. She found these races fascinating too, and Ernest explained to her about each rider and the air pull from the lead cycle and who was the favorite and why.

Their interest in bicycle riding extended, too, to the Tour de France and they would sometimes go out to some town or village and watch the riders come through, panting heavily up the hills and racing down them on the other side. They came upon a little village once where some sort of a festival seemed to be going on. They were welcomed by the villagers and soon were invited to enter a beer-drinking contest. Hadley asserted that it was she who won it. The prize was a cow. Replete with beer, Hadley naturally fell asleep on the grass under a tree, and Ernest was left to handle matters. With flowery speeches and much mutal admiration, he managed to persuade the villagers that they should award the prize to somebody else. Of course it would have been different if a cow was something you could ride, Hadley remarked.

In spite of all this activity, Ernest was working hard and productively. They did not often stay out late in the evenings, for Marie Cocotte had to go home to her husband and could only occasionally stay overnight and Hadley did not like to leave the baby alone. If they did leave him, they would ask Madame Chautard downstairs to keep an ear open in case the child woke up, which he rarely did. Kitty Cannell had given them a cat, which they called Feather Puss. He was Bumby's good friend, and Ernest thought he was the best baby-sitter possible.

One evening they went to a concert given by an aspiring young composer-pianist who played some of his own works. Characteristically, Ernest gave his own opinion of the performance when, in a sudden pause, his voice boomed out: "I like my Stravinsky straight!" When they got home, Hadley was furious to discover that Madame Chautard had wakened the baby, brought him down to her apartment, and was amusing a roomful of guests with him.

Paris winters can be rainy and cold, and when both Hadley and Bumby came down with bad colds they wished they could go to Switzerland again. They had indulged themselves, however, by going to Pamplona during the summer, which they had enjoyed more than ever, and now their finances were in an almost critical state. They were elated when they heard about the Pension Taube, at Schruns in the Austrian Voralberg, and discovered that they could all three live there for an absurdly low sum and might even make money by subletting their Paris apartment.

Schruns was a charming village, and the Taube was a comfortable, simple, homelike place. The food was hearty and plentiful, and there were thirty-six kinds of beer. In addition there was a beautiful, healthy, energetic young Austrian girl, named Mathilde Braun and called Tiddy, who was ready to care for Bumby. There was even a piano for Hadley. Bumby had a room to himself right next to theirs and Hadley would leave in the mornings so that Ernest could work alone. It was fun having a warm place in which to play the piano and to be able to practice regularly every morning while Tiddy, probably flirting with her beau, Maxili, was outside with Bumby, who flourished in the fine mountain air. Bumby soon became Bumbili and Ernest liked to call him *Bumby-schatz*.

There was a large porcelain stove in every room, and at dawn someone would come in with a few burning faggots and light it. Breakfast was served in bed, which was a great luxury. Hadley remembered she had to jump up rapidly once after Ernest, in a fit of pique, flung a butterball which stuck on the ceiling right over her head. It was all very easy living with plenty of good food and red wine, pleasant people around, and Bumby wonderfully taken care of.

They did a lot of skiiing. Walther Lent, who had a ski school, took them up twice to the high mountains for an excursion of several days. Lent was extremely strict and serious and as all the food and supplies had to be carried up in packs, he checked everybody's rucksack before starting out. Hadley had a hard time to keep from smiling on one occasion when Herr Lent discovered that her English friend, Dorothy Johnston, who had joined them at Schruns, had put in a lemon to cheer up the anticipated many cups of tea which was all they were going to drink. "We're not going to carry any superfluous luggage," Lent declared, removing the lemon. Dorothy, of course, managed to sneak one along anyway. She was a great friend of Hadley's, a quiet, gentle person but with a hard core of determination. Ernest thought she was taking up too much of Hadley's time, but Hadley enjoyed the companionship during the long periods when Ernest would be working.

Ernest had long since grown a moustache, but at Schruns he let his beard grow too, which Hadley thought "quite good-looking, quite fierce-looking." The peasants in the mountains called him "The Black Christ," and some of them, who came down to the local Bierstube varied it with "The Black Kirsch-drinking Christ." [10]

They were outdoors a lot and were strong and healthy, and in the evenings they would come back to a hot supper in the big room with the bar at one end and everyone all together. Bumby ate with them and then went cozily to bed. Keeping house at the sawmill apartment in Paris had been far from easy, and Hadley thoroughly enjoyed the comfort and freedom from domestic burdens at the Pension Taube.

Ernest would sometimes play poker with some of the local gentry, although gambling was illegal, but as one of the regulars was captain of the *Gendarmerie* no one worried too much. There was a supply of good books that Sylvia Beach had let them take, and Hadley knitted warm scarves and sweaters and caps for Ernest and Bumby from the slightly fat natural wool that never got wet.

It was a wonderful, peaceful, happy winter, clixamed at the end by the great news that Ernest's book of short stories, *In Our Time*, had been accepted for publication by Boni and Liveright in New York.

CHAPTER

VII

THEY WERE GLAD to get back to the pace and excitement of Paris that spring of 1925, to see all their friends again, to sit under the trees at the Closerie des Lilas, to be welcomed back at the Nègre de Toulouse. Ernest had sold a long story to Ernest Walsh's new magazine, *This Quarter*, and had actually been paid for it. He had also been approached about his future work by another editor, Maxwell Perkins of Scribner's, who had become interested through Scott Fitzgerald's praise of Ernest's writing.

The Paris crowd of Americans, visitors and expatriates alike, was constantly growing. They felt that Paris was the center of creative activity and they wanted to share in it. Ernest was a forceful attraction. He was no longer simply a powerful young man with great potential. He had begun to arrive. And that was when "the rich," as both Hemingway and Hadley later described them, began to move in.

It was a worldly crowd, full of intellectual and artistic ferment, some of it real, some of it bogus, some of them obsessed with their own egos, a few of them deeply and sincerely interested in Ernest's talent. The Hemingways' finances were as restricted as ever, but these people "could offer them all the amenities, could take them anywhere for gorgeous meals," could

produce any kind of entertainment and diversion. Although
Ernest accepted it all, Hadley thought that he resented it and always kept "a very stiff upper front to satisfy himself." He did
not want "simply to sink back and take all this," but the success
and admiration was heady stuff and he could not help but enjoy
it.[1] Hadley used to be wryly amused when Ernest and Gertrude
Stein would talk about worldly success and how it did not mean
anything to them.[2] The fact that this was true for a part of him,
and that he despised anything false or pretentious, was a source
of inner conflict which sometimes expressed itself in malice.

Later that spring the flamboyant Scott Fitzgeralds burst onto
the Paris scene with their charm and antics and tragic frenetic
aura. Hadley thought Scott "absolutely fascinating," but she was
completely impervious to his charm as she had "too fascinating
a husband" of her own. She enjoyed Zelda's lovely appearance
but was somewhat put off by her frivolity. Both the Fitzgeralds
would look exhausted after a night on the town, and Zelda would
be surprised that Hadley, having gone to bed at a reasonable
hour, would seem so fresh. They had an annoying habit of ar-
riving at some hour like four in the morning full of childish nonsense, and it was "hard to be enthusiastic about them then." [3]

Among other new friends the Hemingways made that year
were Gerald and Sara Murphy, a charming couple with three
children who had moved to France some years earlier to escape
what they felt was the stuffy and bigoted life in America. They
had a gift for living, and ample funds with which to indulge
their tastes. Penetrating and discriminating connoisseurs, their
homes in Paris and at Cap d'Antibes in the south of France became a meeting place for artists and writers. Their warm hospitality and affectionate interest in their friends and their idyllic
family life had a very special quality. It was a little precious perhaps, a little too perfect, a delicate savoring of life which was the

antithesis of Hemingway's intense, direct involvement in everything he did.

In spite of Hadley's conviction that Ernest made a marvelous impression wherever he went, his quality did not always make itself felt and one person who was very much put off him at first was Pauline Pfeiffer. She had moved to Paris with her younger sister, Jinny, to work for *Vogue* magazine. Pauline had been brought up in St. Louis and attended school there at the Visitation Convent not far from where Hadley used to live. The two sisters wanted to meet the Hemingways, and Kitty Cannell invited them together to her apartment. Although Pauline was only four years younger than Hadley, they had never happened to meet in St. Louis.

Hadley thought Pauline very chic, perfectly groomed, with everything in impeccable taste. She was small and dark, very slim, with hair bobbed almost like a boy's except for thick bangs on her forehead. At this first meeting, Ernest spent most of the time talking with Jinny and liked her much better than her sister. But he was impressed with Pauline's chipmunk coat and said later he would love to take out Jinny if she wore her sister's coat.

Hadley asked the two girls to come some day to see Bumby, and Pauline was even more surprised at the way the Hemingways lived than she had been by Hadley's shabby, out-of-fashion clothes, which she had already noted. Pauline came from a wealthy background and the bare simplicity, if not poverty, of the sawmill apartment and the brief view she had of Ernest lolling unshaven, reading on the bed, appalled her. Like Kitty Cannell, she blamed Ernest for making Hadley live in such a way and did not see how she could put up with it. Hadley did feel awkward sometimes in the company of all these well-dressed women but she had never been vain nor had much interest in clothes except in the way that any young woman likes pretty things. After all, what mattered were Ernest and his work, that

Bumby was flourishing, and to economize to the extreme so that they could do the things they really wanted to do.

Pamplona was one of the things they did not want to miss, and they went once again that summer. Ernest had always been a pacesetter and had the gift of sparking other people's interest in his enthusiasms. Already the previous year a group of friends had accompanied the Hemingways to Pamplona and it had been a great success. A different group came along this time and from the beginning everything somehow did not seem quite right. Ernest and Hadley, their old friend Bill Smith, and Don Stewart had gone ahead for a week's fishing on the Irati River, which they found almost completely destroyed by the spring logging. Pamplona too had changed and was now invaded by the fashionable set seeking new thrills. But the real dislocation came from within their own group of friends, the sex and jealousy that festered scarcely below the surface. It all centered on a striking Englishwoman, Lady Duff Twysden. Hadley thought her wonderfully attractive, a real woman of the world with no sexual inhibitions. Although her companion of the moment was a weak inebriate, Pat Guthrie, she had just spent a week with Harold Loeb, and she obviously was attracted to Ernest, although no one thought, and Hadley agreed, that any actual affair ever developed between them. With all three men present, the strong undercurrents of feeling, and their brief, explosive expressions, formed an ugly distraction to the essential drama of the *feria*. Hadley felt it acutely, although she was not the only one aware of the change. But it had all been frenetically gay.

Hadley and Ernest went on by themselves afterward to Madrid, where they could see more of a brilliant new matador, Niño de la Palma, whom they admired. He singled Hadley out for special attention, dedicating a bull to her and presenting her afterward with the ear. She did not know quite what to do with it and ended up wrapping it in a handkerchief and stuffing it in a bureau drawer. Never having been given an ear before, she kept it long after one could no longer ignore its presence, and Ernest had told her she ought to get rid of it, or, at the very least, cut it up and send pieces of it to her friends.

Ernest started work on a novel almost as soon as they reached Madrid. The whole recent Pamplona experience was simmering inside him and had to be written out. From Madrid they went to Valencia and then across the border to Hendaye, where Hadley left Ernest to go on to Paris to get the apartment ready and to greet Bumby. The child had been staying with Marie Cocotte and her husband in Britanny. Hadley missed him and worried about him, though she knew he was in the best of hands with Marie and her husband, Ton-Ton, an ex-soldier who could tell stories and knew all there was to know about the Napoleonic Wars.

Ernest followed a week later and continued to work on his book as even he had never worked before. He was exhausted when he finished it toward the end of September, a bare two months after he had begun. It was during a short trip to Chartres that he finally decided on the title: *The Sun Also Rises.* Hadley was happy and excited and thought the book magnificent.

They took up again the usual round of life in Paris and saw a great deal of all their friends. Although Hadley felt that Ernest was the real attraction, she did realize that everyone thought that they made a good team and that theirs was a "nice home to come to." Ernest showed that he was proud of her and made her feel as though he was always saying, in effect, "See, here is this beautiful, smart, talented, charming wife of mine," and he wanted her to share in everything. Although there were obviously plenty of people who were very fond of Hadley for herself, she was always aware of the brilliance of her partner.[4]

Ernest wanted to surprise Hadley with a very special present for her thirty-fourth birthday. They had met and admired a

Spanish painter, Joan Miro, a small man whom Hadley remembered as having perfectly round blue eyes. There was one of his paintings that they specially liked, "The Farm," and Ernest hoped to be able to acquire it for Hadley. He threw dice for the chance to buy it with a friend who had persuaded the painter to part with it, but when he won he had to borrow money all over Paris to pay for it, earning more criticisms from various friends who wondered how he could spend money on a painting when Hadley needed so many basic essentials. But Hadley had no such complaints at all. She was thrilled with the painting and hung it over their bed. She felt that Miro never painted anything equal to it before or since.

When Ernest's book of short stories, *In Our Time*, appeared that early winter, most of the reviews were favorable, but Ernest was irritated by a comment that compared him to Sherwood Anderson. He promptly sat down to write something that he hoped would end this kind of comparison of his work. He called it *The Torrents of Spring*, and it was an obvious and unkind parody of Anderson's latest book, *Dark Laughter*. Hemingway had often before vented his feelings against people on paper, but Hadley hoped that he could be persuaded to put this manuscript away unpublished. She thought it needlessly cruel to someone who had been so very good to them both, especially to Ernest. Most of their friends agreed with her. But there was one who did not. That was Pauline Pfeiffer, who had long since discovered the mistake she had made in her negative first impression of Ernest. She was enthusiastic about *The Torrents of Spring*, and urged Ernest to submit it for publication. Hadley always thought he might not have done so without Pauline's persuasion, and she sympathized deeply with Anderson's hurt and bewilderment when the book finally did appear.[5]

It was Schruns again that December, where Ernest arrived with a heavy cold. He was subject to attacks of laryngitis which were considered hazardous to him, or at least he convinced Hadley that they were. She remembered that he seemed worried at these times about a possible attack of angina, to which his father was subject. He told her he had had such an attack after he was wounded in Italy and that it could kill him if it recurred. Nothing then or later showed that Hemingway ever had angina, and his tremendous physical activity all his life would contradict such a possibility. It was not in connection with physical exertion that he spoke of it to Hadley but only when he was ill, and she had to take very good care of him at those times.[6] He stayed in bed at Schruns, basking in the attention, writing letters and feeling pleasantly sorry for himself.

He was well on the way to recovery and had started work on the revision of *The Sun Also Rises* when Pauline Pfeiffer arrived to spend the Christmas holidays. The malicious gossip in Paris had been that the Pfeiffer girls had come abroad to find husbands. Pauline, at least, had decided who that husband was to be. By now she had fallen in love with Ernest Hemingway and had made up her mind that he was her man. It wasn't difficult. Hadley knew, of course, even before the first boat trip on the *Leopoldina*, that girls "had a habit of falling in love with Ernest," but she also knew that he loved her, and she loved him. He flirted, naturally, and so did she occasionally, but their flirtations had never gone further than that. Pauline made a point of being companionable and friendly with Hadley, almost as though she were the focus of interest. Hadley had no suspicion at all that there was anything more in Pauline's calculations.

Pauline was back in Paris in January 1926, when Ernest stopped off there for a few days on his way to New York where he was going to make the final arrangements for changing publishers to Scribner's. Pauline kept up the pretense of the innocent happy threesome, writing Hadley, who had stayed behind at Schruns, all about what she and Ernest were doing, the exhibit of paintings they were going to and how splendid Ernest was. She did not mention, nor did Ernest, how her relationship with Ernest had developed and that not only was she in love with him but that by now he was completely infatuated with her too. Many years later Hemingway wrote poignantly and bitterly of his tearing feeling of guilt at his betrayal of Hadley whom he still loved, who was and always would be a part of him.

Hadley waited impatiently at Schruns for his return from his visit to New York, where he stayed for nearly three weeks. She wrote her friend, Isabelle Simmons, that she had climbed every mountain and was even tired of the Bach-Busoni Chaconne which she was working on "to gladden the ear of Hemingstein on his return." Ernest's return boat had been delayed and she was in despair wondering how she could wait the few more days until it landed to have her *liebling* back. And then, she realized, he would have to stop off in Paris for money and to do something about the apartment. She did not know then or later that he would pass up three trains he might have taken, in order to be with Pauline. But Hadley's mood was very dark. Perhaps it was a premonition of the sorrow that lay ahead.[7]

Long afterward Ernest wrote about how he felt when he arrived finally at the little station at Schruns and saw Hadley, lovelier than ever, with Bumby by her side, and wished he had died before loving anyone esle.[8] They were together again, complete and happy. They skiied, and played with Bumby, and had good friends and good dinners in the cozy dining room and sang songs with the patrons of the bar at the end of the long room and Ernest worked well and hard and finished his revision of the book. Sara and Gerald Murphy came with John Dos Passos for a short visit. Everything seemed safe and secure again.

Back in Paris that spring, however, the affair with Pauline began again. Still trying to maintain the deception, she and her sister Jinny invited Hadley for a motor trip to the Chateau country. Hadley looked forward to this as a refreshing change as Ernest and she "never went anywhere except to fish or to ski." It all started off well with Jinny driving and Hadley happy and interested in what they were going to see. It was not long, however, before she was struck with how bad-tempered Pauline was. She seemed to snap at every remark or else withdraw into moody silence. Hadley naturally was hurt by this, and although they did see some sights and visit some lovely chateaux, Hadley was not particularly enjoying herself. One night she asked Jinny, whom she knew was very close to her sister, whether she thought that "Pauline and Ernest got along together awfully well," or some such question. Jinny's answer really gave her a shock. "Oh, well, I think they're very fond of each other," she told Hadley. It was not the words Jinny used as much as the inflection of her voice which put Hadley on her guard. It really gave her pause and it was she who was moody for the rest of the trip. She still felt that it was extremely kind of Pauline and Jinny to have taken her on the excursion, but she wondered later if the real purpose behind it had been to reveal the truth to her. She felt that she had been "terribly innocent" about it all or "just plain dumb," for she truly had suspected nothing until Jinny's remark.[9]

When she got back to Paris she confronted Ernest with her suspicions. And he was furious. He did not attempt to deny anything but he behaved as though it were Hadley who was at fault for having mentioned the matter and that everything would have been all right if only she had not brought it into the open. There was no idea of a break between them, and he seemed to feel that everything could and should go on as before.

Pauline sent a meassage to Hadley through Ernest that she would like to talk with her, but Hadley turned the offer down. Pauline was one of those people who was quick and smart and clever and she would be full of quick and smart and clever explanations, Hadley felt, and "would get the better of her." She did not think anything could come of such a talk. After all, it was between Ernest and herself. He continued to assume that they could simply continue as they had been doing.[10]

Hadley gave it a sincere, and extremely painful try. The Murphys had invited them to visit at Cap d'Antibes, and Hadley went down there with Bumby, who had a bad cough which had prevented them from accompanying Ernest to Madrid, where he found unseasonable cold and the bullfights cancelled. Pauline was in Italy visiting her wealthy uncle.

Bumby's cough seemed suspicious to the Murphys and when it was diagnosed as whooping cough, they became almost frantic with worry for their own children. The doctor said Bumby should be quarantined, and Hadley had to find a place to move to with him. She was very grateful when the Scott Fitzgeralds proposed a solution. They had just rented a large villa with a private beach, and the lease on a smaller one they had been occupying had not yet run out, so they offered it to Hadley. She sent for Marie Cocotte to come and help her with Bumby, and in a few days Ernest arrived from Spain. Every evening, Hadley recalled, a whole carful would come over, the Murphys, the MacLeishes, the Fitzgeralds, and whatever other visitors there might be. They would arrive just at cocktail time, bringing refreshments, and would park in the road. Hadley and Ernest would sit out on the little verandah and they would all talk back and forth across the tiny grass plot that separated them. There was a spiked fence between the house and the street and before their stay was over all those spikes were covered by upside down empty bottles.

Young as he was, some of these friends started calling Ernest "Papa," picking it up perhaps from Bumby, and Ernest enjoyed it very much. Hadley felt that he always had a protective feeling toward people, even when, like Gerald Murphy, they were a good deal older than he. He "wanted people to look up to him as

a sort of protector," she thought, and felt it was a "very affectionate name, a noble name, almost like a title, and it took like
mad until he became 'Papa' to everyone." [11]

One person who did not worry in the least about the quaran-
tine was Pauline, who came over from Italy and moved into the
villa with the Hemingways, asserting that she had had whooping
cough and was thus immune. Hadley surmised that Ernest had
written Pauline a pathetic letter depicting their isolation, and
Pauline arrived full of determination to add to the general gaiety.
Understandably Hadley hardly felt very gay.

When the lease on the villa ran out, Pauline moved with them
to a small hotel in Juan-les-Pins where Bumby and Marie Cocotte lived in a summerhouse on the grounds. Pauline was ever
present. Everything was done à trois. They would all go to the
beach in the morning, where Pauline insisted on teaching Hadley
to dive and almost killed her in the attempt, as Hadley's childhood back injury made it difficult for her. Ernest and Pauline
wanted Hadley to learn to play bridge, which she really did not
like, and it was hardly surprising that she could not keep her
mind on it. The one pleasure was the long bicycle rides. They
would go for hours, all around the Golfe de Juan, and Hadley
would come back relaxed and blooming and everybody told her
she looked "just the way a young wife should look, rosy cheeks,
clear eyes, strong muscles and everything." [12]

In spite of the fact that everyone was very kind to her, Hadley
imagined that one or two of them, especially Sara Murphy,
sympathized with Ernest and Pauline and may have been critical
of her. And they all made a point of telling her how much they
adored Ernest. Hadley felt at a disadvantage with Pauline whose
smart clothes and well groomed appearance made her feel more
dowdy than ever in comparison.

Hadley did her best not to show how hurt and unhappy she
was, at least in front of Pauline. Although she resented Pauline

and was shocked at her callously close and constant presence, she felt helpless to do anything about it. She sensed that if she told Ernest that Pauline should spend her vacation somewhere else and ought to leave, he would probably go with her. Her role had always been the feminine one, ready to do whatever Ernest wanted. She could not imagine dictating to him, and she knew he would not put up with it.

Hadley did not completely suppress her feelings of resentment, however. In spite of the difficult and even intolerable circumstances, she did not lose her sense of the absurd, and she found all kinds of things she thought hilariously funny coming into her mind. But they had a sharp bite, a bitter edge. Ernest and Pauline did not find them amusing.[13]

Hadley found it incomprehensible that Ernest would put her in the position he had. He had always been kind and considerate, aware of her feelings, and he had never hurt her before or done anything to her that was insensitive or cruel. It was perhaps this that made her realize the seriousness of what was going on between him and Pauline, although Ernest still maintained the attitude that everything should continue as before. If there was one thing that Hadley did not relish, however, it was the position of the wronged wife, and nothing that Ernest was doing made her "fall any harder in love with him." The longer the situation continued the more angry she became and, strangely enough, she was aware that she began to feel a little relieved too. "I certainly felt alternate relief and rage," she remembered later.[14]

It seemed to Hadley that it dragged on for an eternity, though actually they were on the Riviera for only about a month. She was glad when they went off to Pamplona in July with the Murphys and, of course, Pauline, whose vacation was about to end. After the *feria*, Pauline returned to Paris, and Ernest and Hadley went off to San Sebastian and Madrid, by themselves at last. Pauline kept besieging them with letters, however, telling

them of all she was doing and going to do and saying she hoped
for letters from them, especially from Hadley. But Hadley by
now had had enough.

The Hemingways' trip back to Paris was to be their last together, for Hadley moved directly into a small hotel near the
Closerie des Lilas, and Ernest accepted Gerald Murphy's offer
of his studio. Bitterly unhappy as it all was, Hadley found a
separation easier to bear than remaining together, knowing the
affair with Pauline was going on. The break-up came as a shock
to their friends. Many of them believed that Pauline had behaved very badly toward Hadley, pursuing Ernest with a ruth-
less tenacity. Long afterward, Hadley shrugged this off. "Well,
they were in love," she observed.[15]

Hadley knew how impressionable Ernest was and thought he
was "almost weak" in the sense that he was always very touched
and reacted tenderly if somebody loved him whether he himself
was in love or not. And so she laid out a final test for him and
Pauline. "I might have been the Emperor Tiberius," she commented later. They should not see each other for a hundred days
and if, at the end of that time, they were still in love, she would
divorce Ernest.[16]

Pauline and Ernest decided the only way that they could hold
to this was for Pauline to leave for America, which she did. But
she wrote him almost every day, and Ernest would visit Hadley
with detailed accounts of how Pauline was suffering for lack
of him. Hadley recalled that she felt she was being "terribly
mean," and was glad to remember that she had, in the end, not
stuck to the hundred days ultimatum.

It was from Chartres, where Hadley had gone for a few days,
leaving Bumby in his father's care, that she wrote Ernest that
he should look into ways and means of getting a divorce, since
he evidently wanted one. He answered her with a wonderfully
grateful, glowing letter extolling her generosity, her courage,

her loyalty, her unfailing loving and self-sacrificing support of him always. *The Sun Also Rises* bore the dedication: "This book is for Hadley and John Hadley Nicanor." He arranged for Hadley to receive all the royalties from it. And he set up a trust fund for Bumby. The bitter period of conflict between them was over and much of what had been fine and good between them would remain.

Hadley was no longer the very shy, unsure young woman who had come to Paris nearly five years before. She went often in the mornings to the Closerie des Lilas, while Bumby was in kindergarten, and was amused at the people who would turn up there "just dying of curiosity" as to exactly what had happened between her and Ernest.

She found an apartment for herself and Bumby, and F. Puss the cat, at 35, rue de Fleurus, not far from Gertrude Stein. She recalled wryly that she made Ernest go to the apartment above the sawmill with one of the handcarts used for moving things in Paris and take out some of her possessions, things that had been in her mother's house: the heavy family silver that her brother Jamie had given her as a wedding present, the lovely Dresden plates of which she was so fond. She had treasured the teapot that went with that set and had never let Marie Cocotte wash it but did that herself and, of course, in the end had broken it. But there were lots of other things and it took Ernest several trips to deliver them all, including the Miro painting he had given her for her birthday the year before. He trundled the loads over to her new apartment, "weeping down the street and I know he was very sorry for himself," she remembered. But she thought he enjoyed this self-pity. Hadley felt sorry for him too, for although she knew that he and Pauline were in love, she recognized that he was wracked with guilt and remorse about her.

The divorce went through in Paris in January, 1927. It was all now formally over, at least for Hadley. For Ernest and

Pauline the situation was a little different. Pauline was an ardent
Catholic and they had to follow a rather tortuous path to explain
that Ernest had been baptized years before by a priest as he lay
with other wounded in Italy, and as his marriage to Hadley had
not taken place in the Church, it was therefore not valid. A
great many of their friends sympathized with Hadley at the idea
that, "If you weren't a Catholic and had been married in a little
Methodist Church in Michigan, it wasn't a real marriage." [17]

The process of separation had been extremely painful and difficult, but in the end Hadley was in a way relieved at being on
her own again. She had always felt that being married to Ernest
was a great responsibility and a demanding one. She was profoundly aware of what an unusual and extraordinary person he
was, but she was not too much worried about Ernest now, for
she felt that Pauline would make him a good wife. She decided
Pauline was tougher and more resilient than she and perhaps
better able to keep up with the pace and intensity of Ernest's
life. Pauline was interested in his work, and ambitious for him
too, and could do a great many things for him financially which
Hadley, with her small inheritance, had not been able to do. Sad
as it all was, Hadley found that now she felt in a strange way
"released." As she recalled later, "I didn't know what was going
to happen to me, but I had lots of confidence in myself and
plenty of friends both at home and abroad. I knew that I could
get along and I knew that I could still get some fun out of music.
And we divided Bumby." [18]

Marie Cocotte came for five hours every day and took Bumby
to his kindergarten. When Hadley wanted to go out in the
evening, there was a ready baby-sitter, Manuel Komroff, a Russian who liked to spend quiet evenings in the cozy, warm apartment, writing and relaxing. Just across the street was a friend of
Hadley's who was convalescing from a severe illness. He too had
just been divorced, so they had that in common, and they en-

joyed each other's company and had a good time gossiping about everyone.

In April, Hadley decided to go home for a visit, to see her friends and family and to show off Bumby, who was a handsome, sturdy little boy of whom she was very proud. Everybody had been prepared to meet a broken-hearted woman, but Hadley was "feeling like a million dollars and free as air." [19] Even when she heard in May that Ernest and Pauline had finally been married, her mood of gaiety did not break.

She stopped off first in New York for a visit with the mother of one of her old Bryn Mawr friends, and she went to parties and theaters. From there she went to St. Louis to stay with her sister and took Bumby around to all her old friends and schoolteachers and he was much admired by everyone. She paid a short visit to Oak Park so that Dr. and Mrs. Hemingway could see their grandson, and she was touched by Dr. Hemingway's delight in the boy. Hadley thought he took him to see nearly every family in the whole town. She was aware, however, at how distressed the Hemingways were at the divorce.

Hadley had not seen the George Blackman family for a good many years, but the memory of them and all they had represented to her in her early days was as strong as ever. They were still living in Carmel, California where they had moved after leaving St. Louis, and Hadley spent the rest of the summer near them in Carmel. Her former piano teacher, Harrison Williams, was there too with his wife, and several other old St. Louis friends. It was a fine relaxed summer. The Blackmans were as charming and affectionate as ever. The country was lovely, the climate perfect, and there were plenty of friends, new and old. But Hadley was never tempted for a moment to put down roots there. Nor did she have any desire to return and settle down in St. Louis. She had found her sister Fonnie affectionate and concerned, but the last thing Hadley wanted to do was to go back to the old, restricted life. It was in Paris that she had really found herself and blossomed in every way. She knew how to live there and felt more at home in Paris than she did anywhere else.

VIII

John dos passos once wrote that Ernest Hemingway left his wives "more able to cope with life than he found them." [1] This was certainly true in Hadley's case. The timid, unhappy girl her mother looked upon as "an invalid who shouldn't even spend a night alone," had blossomed into an independent, self-confident young woman who knew not only how to deal with life but how to enjoy it. Her interests had increased, her vision and understanding had deepened, but most of all Ernest had given her a belief in herself. She had thought her happiness dependent on Ernest, and for a long time it was, but after the divorce she found she was able to function successfully on her own.

Back in Paris, that October of 1927, Hadley set about re-establishing her life. She found an apartment on the rue Auguste-Blanqui. Marie Cocotte, as always, ran the ménage and helped look out for Bumby. Ernest, who came occasionally to pick up the boy for a visit, thought Hadley looked beautiful, in some contrast to Pauline who was having a difficult time with her first pregnancy.

At thirty-six, Hadley was more attractive than she had ever been. If her life now lacked the color and excitement she had known with Ernest, it was nevertheless agreeable. She could go at her own pace, and develop her own interests. She loved to dance, she played tennis at the club on the Boulevard Arago, and she made many new friends. Among them was one in particular who appealed to her. He was Paul Scott Mowrer.

They had met for the first time by chance through mutual friends in the spring of 1927 shortly after Hadley's divorce. It was surprising they had not seen each other before for Paul had been living in Paris for some seventeen years, first as Paris correspondent for the *Chicago Daily News*, later as European head of its foreign service. He and Ernest had known each other casually, meeting occasionally at the Anglo-American Press Club, but Hadley had not met Paul then. She had heard about him, however, and once asked Ernest what he was like. "A little too saintly for me," Ernest growled. He was to change this opinion later when he got to know Paul better.[2]

Paul Mowrer could be deceptive at first meeting. He was an unusual man. On the one hand, he was a highly experienced, brilliant journalist and political writer, author of several books on world politics and recipient of the first Pulitzer Prize ever awarded for foreign correspondence. On the other hand, he was a subtle, imaginative, and prolific poet.

Paul and Hadley liked each other at once but their deeper feelings for each other developed only gradually. At the age of twenty-two, in 1910, Paul had married Winifred Adams, but during the years they had grown apart. Though remaining excellent friends, their lives had diverged almost completely. Their two boys were nearly grown, and would soon return to America to finish their education.

Paul Mowrer had the kind of subtle face and personality that Hadley had thought she would have preferred to Ernest's on the occasion of their first meeting. He was her kind of person. Ernest had so many qualities that she admired profoundly, and she felt she had been lucky to have the capacity to appreciate him, but much as she had loved him, there were some manifestations of his personality she had had to get used to. She did not ever feel that way with Paul. She loved his quiet ways, his solidly based knowledge of so many subjects, his profound modesty. She used to laugh at the way Ernest would go right through every door ahead of her, wanting to be "Johnny on the spot in every situation." It was not important but was indicative of his instinct "to get everywhere first" and it used to leave her wondering what to do, "Shall I stay behind or move forward?" [3]

There was never anything like that with Paul. She liked to watch him make his way with people unobtrusively, with an impact all the more effective because it was so subtly and gracefully executed.

When Paul first realized how serious the relationship between him and Hadley was getting, he made a point of seeing and talking frankly with Ernest, stating his intention to marry Hadley. For the first time since their divorce, Ernest's feelings of guilt toward Hadley were assuaged. He had come to know Paul better, and to like and admire him, and he was enormously relieved that Hadley's future would be in such good hands. Bumby too was delighted. When he learned that Paul and his mother were to be married, he commented happily, "Oh, he's one of my very best friends." [4]

Paul and Hadley were married on July 3, 1933, in a quiet ceremony at the Registry Office in London where Paul was covering the World Economic Conference. Afterwards, Mrs. Bullard, later Lady Salter, gave a reception at the Hotel Connaught, attended by many of Paul's colleagues and diplomat friends from the Conference. There had been many delays along the way, Paul's divorce, a *de jure* recognition of a *de facto* situation, and the need to be absolutely sure that they wanted to spend the rest of their lives together.

A few weeks later when they were back in Paris, it was suggested that Paul return to Chicago as chief editorial writer of the *Daily News*, with the promise of the editorship of the paper soon after. He talked it over with Hadley and the more they discussed it, the happier they were at the idea. Both of them had been away from home for a long time, and it would be good for Bumby to go to school in America. Not quite six months after their marriage, they started for home.

Life with Paul was all that Hadley had dreamed it would be. In spite of his heavy responsibilities and busy schedule, there was always about him a feeling of repose, of tranquility, a great contrast to Ernest's intensity and moodiness. Paul had great inner resources, a rare sense of humor, and a broad range of intellectual and artistic interests. He loved nature and birds, and knew all about them, and was an ardent fisherman, something Hadley thought Hemingway had introduced him to. He liked to play chess and his favorite partner was his brother, Edgar Ansel Mowrer, also a Pulitzer Prize winner, eminent foreign correspondent, and author. Their chess game spanned a lifetime and the world, and when they were separated, which was most of the time and often by continents, they carried on their games regularly by letter, telephone or cable.

The relationship between Hemingway and the Mowrers was very friendly. Bumby, now called Jack, spent a great part of his vacations with his father, and Hadley was pleased that Pauline made no distinction between him and her own two sons. Although Hadley and Ernest did not meet, they corresponded occasionally, not only about Jack, but as old friends who were concerned about each other's lives and happiness. She would write him about what she and Paul were doing, and the new house they were building at Lake Bluff, and Ernest looked forward to seeing them some time in the fine new place. He would tell her about his travels and the adventures he had in Spain during the war there. He was solicitous about Jack's expenses and sent her money regularly for his education from the trust fund he had set up. He had arranged that if anything happened to him, Pauline would send all the trust papers to Hadley. Not that he was expecting anything, he said, but liked to be tidy about such things. He told her of a play he was writing which he hoped was good. He always sent greetings to Paul for whom he had much admiration. When he was working on his novel, *For Whom the Bell Tolls*, he reported how far it had progressed and said he had never worked harder or more steadily. He gave her news of old friends told her of all the fish he had caught.[5]

One summer the Mowrers were vacationing at a ranch out West. They had spent the day at a nearby lake fishing for grayling. They had just finished and were starting up the path when they met Ernest coming down it. He had come to pick up Jack and had been told at the ranch where he could find them. It had been ten years since they had seen each other, and the reunion was a happy one. Ernest had much news. War had just broken out in Europe.[6] Ernest wrote later saying how handsome he thought Paul and Hadley were. He couldn't have done better if he had invented them.[7]

Later the war brought anxious days for them all. Jack, after parachuting into France for the OSS, was reported missing in action. It was a long time before word came through that he was wounded, a prisoner, but at least he was alive. Ernest kept Hadley informed of everything he could find out about their son who was finally liberated after months in prison camps.

Paul resigned from the *Daily News* in 1944, but he was not yet ready for retirement. There was far too much going on. When he was offered the chance of returning to France as foreign correspondent for the *New York Post*, the war was not yet over. Leaving Hadley to dispose of the house at Lake Bluff and pack up all their belongings, he set off at once. Ernest told Hadley not to worry about Paul and sympathized with her for having to leave such a lovely house and told her he always hated leaving anywhere.[8] Within a few months, after the Allied victory, Hadley joined Paul in Paris.

Life in war-torn Paris was very different than it had been in the twenties. Food everywhere was short and it was a long time before a commissary was set up for businessmen and newsmen. Paul was asked to set up a Paris edition of the *Post*. The paper was started primarily for the thousands of American soldiers who were in France and it continued until the great mass of them had gone home. Soon after the Paris edition of the *Post* closed down, Paul and Hadley decided to return to America for good.

Paul had really retired now, and they thought very carefully about where in the United States they would settle. Hadley remembered nostalgically the summers of her early years. Paul had never been north of Boston but he fell in love with New England at once. They bought an old house at Chocorua, New Hampshire. It had a fine view of Chocorua Mountain, which reminded Hadley of the Matterhorn. There were woods to walk in, and a group of interesting neighbors. Paul could now settle down to his real love—writing poetry. There would be plenty of good books and good recordings. Hadley would have a piano and friends to play duets with. And they could read, and walk, and watch the birds, and fish in the mountain streams, and there was no one to please but themselves.

Later they started going during the severe part of the winters to Florida. They did not choose the resorts and beach areas but quiet places well off the beaten tourist track—along the Kissimmee River where the air was soft and the fishing was good; down in the Everglades, with its rich soil and wildlife refuges. It was at Canal Point on Lake Okeechobee that they finally found their real winter home in a small cottage on the grounds of a beautifully landscaped estate. It was peaceful, and Hadley was content.

She found life with Paul about as perfect as it could be. It was at the end of one of those long, quiet winters in Florida that Paul Mowrer died, April 4, 1971.

The last time that Hadley had heard from Ernest Hemingway was in March, 1961. She and Paul were again out West at a ranch when she was called to the phone. To her great surprise it was Ernest. He wanted to ask her if she could recall the name of someone in Paris during their years together, someone who had not treated the younger writers as he should. Hadley was unable to identify to whom or what he was referring. The conversation was very friendly. There was nothing in what he said that was in any way disturbing. And yet, there had been something in his voice that distressed her and when she left the phone, she realized she was in tears. The news of his tragic death came not long afterwards.[9]

Hadley has no bitterness about the break-up of her marriage with Ernest Hemingway. It had been a hard and painful experience, but she knew that in the "long, very long run" it had been for the best.[10] After Pauline and Ernest were divorced, Pauline invited the Mowrers to visit her at Key West, and Hadley was surprised at Pauline's bitterness toward Ernest. She herself could never have felt that way about him, she said. Her years with him had been just right. Everything had been gala with Ernest. Everything had been the greatest fun. And it had ended at just the right time. She had been able to keep up with Ernest's pace, his tremendous vitality, the skiiing, walking, fishing trips, the constant activity, but she felt that she would not have been able to continue that forever. She had loved every minute of their life together, but her real and deepest happiness came in her marriage to Paul.

For Hemingway, those early years with Hadley in Paris always retained a special kind of magic and he often recalled them nostalgically and tenderly in things he wrote and in his letters to

Hadley over the years. There were many people in Hemingway's life whom he later turned against. But never Hadley. He would remember all the things they had done together, the silly poems and songs they had made up for each other which he would sing to himself when he felt particularly lonely. Especially during the break-ups of his marriages to Pauline, and his third wife, Martha Gellhorn, he would think of Hadley, and write her letters signing himself with one of the old nicknames they used to use. The more he saw of other women, he told her, the more he admired her. Maybe things would be better in the hereafter, but perhaps they had already had their share of Heaven in the places they had been to, in the forests of the Dolomites, the Pyrenees and the Black Forest.[11] Sometimes he would lie awake at night remembering all the things they had done, their first visit by themselves to Pamplona, the horse races and even the old *Leopoldina,* the boat that had first brought them to Europe. They were lucky to have had Paris when they were young, he thought, and Paris still seemed to him the loveliest place of all.[12]

For Hadley too, the years with Ernest never lost their aura of enchantment. Many, many years later she would recall Ernest and all they did together and would become gay and animated at the recollection. And often she would say, "he gave me the key to the world."

NOTES

Chapter I

1. Hadley Richardson to Ernest Hemingway, June 4, 1921.
2. HR to EH, June 21, 1921.
3. HR to EH, April 3, 1921.
4. HR to EH, Ibid.
5. HR to EH, June 6, 1921.
6. HR to EH, Ibid.
7. HR to EH, June 20, 1921.
8. HR to EH, July 5, 1921.
9. HR to EH, April 25, 1921.
10. HR to EH, Ibid.

Material for this chapter based on interviews with Hadley Richardson Mowrer November 29, 1970; November 30, 1970; January 6, 1971; January 25, 1972.

Chapter II

1. HR to EH, January 9, 1921.
2. Interview with HRHM, November 30, 1970.
3. HR to EH, January 9, 1921.
4. HR to EH, January 1, 1921.
5. HR to EH, January 12, 1921.
6. HR to EH, January 16, 1921.
7. HR to EH, Thanksgiving Day, 1920.

8. HR to EH, January 7, 1921.
9. HR to EH, February 8, 1921.
10. HR to EH, January 13, 1921.
11. HR to EH, February 8, 1921.
12. HR to EH, January 20, 1921.
13. HR to EH, March 5, 1921.
14. HR to EH, March 7, 1921.
15. HR to EH, March 29, 1921.
16. Interview with HRHM, March 27, 1971.
17. Interview with HRHM, November 30, 1970.
18. HR to EH, March 29, 1921.
19. HR to EH, April 13, 1921.
20. HR to EH, April 20, 1921.
21. HR to EH, April 27, 1921.
22. HR to EH, April 1, 1921.
23. HR to EH, April 16, 1921.
24. HR to EH, April 23, 1921.
25. HR to EH, Ibid.
26. HR to EH, April 27, 1921.
27. HR to EH, January 30, 1921.
28. HR to EH, June 6, 1921.
29. HR to EH, June 10, 1921.
30. HR to EH, April 29, 1921.
31. HR to EH, Undated.
32. Interview with HRHM, November 30, 1970.
33. HR to EH, June 2, 1929.
34. HR to EH, April 3, 1921.
35. HR to EH, June 4, 1921.
36. HR to EH, June 10, 1921.
37. HR to EH, June 5, 1921.

Chapter III

1. HR to EH, June 6, 1921.
2. HR to EH, June 16, 1921.
3. HR to EH, no date.
4. HR to EH, July 5, 1921.
5. HR to EH, July 6, 1921.

6. HR to EH, Ibid.

7. HR to EH, July 7, 1921.

8. HR to EH, July 13, 1921.

9. HR to EH, July 17, 1921.

10. HR to EH, Ibid.

11. HR to Mrs. C.E. Hemingway, July 12, 1921.

12. HR to EH, July 21, 1921.

13. HR to EH, Ibid.

14. HR to EH, July 24, 1921.

15. HR to EH, July 26, 1921.

16. HR to EH, July 19, 1921.

17. HR to EH, August 7, 1921.

18. HR to EH, August 8, 1921.

19. HR to EH, August 18, 1921.

20. HR to EH, Ibid.

21. HR to EH, August 19, 1921.

22. HR to EH, August 22, 1921.

23. HR to EH, August 24, 1921.

24. HR to EH, Ibid.

25. Interview with HRHM, November 30, 1970.

26. Interview with HRHM, November 30, 1970.

27. HRH to Mrs. C.E. Hemingway, September 22, 1921.

28. HRH to Mrs. C.E. Hemingway, Ibid.

29. Interview with HRHM, November 30, 1972.

30. Interview with HRHM, Ibid.

Chapter IV

1. Interview with HRHM, November 29, 1970.

2. Interview with HRHM, December 6, 1971.

3. Interview with HRHM, November 27, 1971.

4. Interview with HRHM, Ibid.

5. Interview with Lewis Galantière, September 12, 1972.

6. Interview with HRHM, November 30, 1970.

7. Interview with HRHM, January 7, 1971.

8. HRH to Mrs. C.E. Hemingway, February 20, 1922.

9. Interview with HRHM, December 6, 1971.

10. Interview with HRHM, Ibid.

11. HRH to Mrs. C.E. Hemingway, February 20, 1922.
12. Interview with HRHM, November 27, 1971.
13. Interview with HRHM, January 7, 1971.
14. HRH to Mrs. C.E. Hemingway, February 20, 1922.
15. HRH to Mrs. C.E. Hemingway, Ibid.
16. Interview with HRHM, November 30, 1970.
17. Interview with HRHM, January 7, 1971.

Chapter V

1. Ernest Hemingway to William Horne, July 17, 1923.
2. Interview with HRHM, January 7, 1971.
3. HRH to Mrs. C.E. Hemingway, October 5, 1922.
4. Interview with HRHM, November 27, 1971.
5. Interview with HRHM, November 29, 1971.
6. Interview with HRHM, January 4, 1972.
7. HRH to Mrs. C.E. Hemingway, December 11, 1922.
8. Interview with HRHM, January 15, 1971.
9. Interview with HRHM, November 27, 1971.
10. Interview with HRHM, January 15, 1971.
11. Interview with HRHM, December 6, 1971.

Chapter VI

1. HRH to Mrs. C.E. Hemingway, September 27, 1923.
2. Hadley Richardson Hemingway to Isabelle Simmons, October 13, 1923.
3. HRH to Dr. and Mrs. C.E. Hemingway, October 18, 1923.
4. Hadley Richardson Hemingway to Isabelle Simmons, October 13, 1923.
5. Interview with HRHM, November 11, 1971.
6. HRH to Mrs. C.E. Hemingway, January 2, 1924.
7. HRH to Mrs. C.E. Hemingway, February 20, 1924.
8. Interview with HRHM, January 6, 1971.
9. Interview with HRHM, January 7, 1972.
10. Interview with HRHM, January 15, 1971.

Chapter VII

1. Interview with HRHM, January 7, 1972.
2. Interview with HRHM, January 6, 1971.
3. Interview with HRHM, January 8, 1971.
4. Interview with HRHM, Ibid.; January 12, 1972.
5. Interview with HRHM, January 8, 1971; November 29, 1971.
6. Interview with HRHM, January 12, 1972; February 4, 1972; January 6, 1971.
7. Hadley Richardson Hemginway to Isabelle Simmons, March 1, 1926.
8. Ernest Hemingway, *The Moveable Feast.*
9. Interview with HRHM, November 29, 1970.
10. Interview with HRHM, Ibid.
11. Interview with HRHM, January 12, 1972.
12. Interview with HRHM, January 8, 1971.
13. Interview with HRHM, January 15, 1971; January 12, 1972.
14. Interview with HRHM, November 29, 1971.
15. Interview with HRHM, February 4, 1972.
16. Interview with HRHM, January 15, 1971.
17. Interview with HRHM, January 7, 1971.
18. Interview with HRHM, November 11, 1971.
19. Interview with HRHM, January 8, 1971.

Chapter VIII

1. John Dos Passos, *The Best Times.* New York: The New American Library, 1966, p. 143.
2. Interview with HRHM, January 18, 1972.
3. Interview with HRHM, Ibid.
4. Interview with HRHM, January 15, 1971.
5. EH to HRHM, January 31, 1938; November 28, 1928; July 15, 1939.
6. Interview with HRHM, January 14, 1971.
7. EH to HRHM, December 1, 1939.
8. EH to HRHM, April 24, 1945.

9. Interview with HRHM, December 6, 1971.
10. Interview with HRHM, January 6, 1971.
11. EH to HRHM, July 26, 1939.
12. EH to HRHM, July 23, 1942; April 24, 1945.

INDEX